The Lockwood High cheer squad has it *all*—sass, looks, and all the right moves. But everything isn't always as perfect as it seems. Because where there's cheer, there's drama. And then there's the ballers—hot, tough, and on point. But what's going to win out—life's pressures or their NFL dreams?

AMIR BALLER *Swag*

Amir Knight has swag, guts, and pure ability.
*But ballin' may not be the future
intended for him ...*

NO HATING

Stephanie Perry Moore
& Derrick Moore

SADDLEBACK
EDUCATIONAL PUBLISHING

BALLER SWAG

All That

No Hating

Do You

Be Real

Got Pride

Copyright © 2012 by Saddleback Educational Publishing
All rights reserved. No part of this book may be reproduced in any form or
by any means, electronic or mechanical, including photocopying, recording,
scanning, or by any information storage and retrieval system, without the written
permission of the publisher. SADDLEBACK EDUCATIONAL PUBLISHING
and any associated logos are trademarks and/or registered trademarks of
Saddleback Educational Publishing.

ISBN-13: 978-1-61651-885-1
ISBN-10: 1-61651-885-5
eBook: 978-1-61247-619-3

Printed in Guangzhou, China
0712/CA21201000

16 15 14 13 12   1 2 3 4 5

To Ann Redding (Mr. Derrick's Mother)

We have always been able to stay in our lane because you have been an example of not hating on others and working hard instead to obtaining for yourself. We hope you know that your prayers have seen us through. What a blessing you have been to our lives. You have shown us how little can become much.

You are a wonderful lady with a big heart ...
we love you!

ACKNOWLEDGEMENTS

When you have talent and shine, sometimes jealous folks may come hating on you. This can make you bitter because they do not know what it took for you to get to where you are. This can make you angry because if they only asked, you could help them achieve greatness as well. This can take some of your joy away, since you have no one to celebrate your success with. However, sometimes you bring the haters because of your bad attitude. You might brag, showboat, or boast. You should be proud of your accomplishments, but always make sure you do not get the big head.

We want you to be confident, but not cocky. Keep working super hard to get even better academically, athletically, and socially. When others are jealous, don't isolate yourself … embrace them. If you are approachable, you can help others elevate their game. The message we want you to comprehend … being a real baller does not mean you set out to be the man. It means because you are dynamic, you make certain everyone around you is better too.

Here is a huge thanks to all those that help us work hard.

To Ms. Stephanie's parents, Dr. Franklin and Shirley Perry Sr., because you are always there, your love allows us to never hate on people with parents who care.

To our publisher, especially Arianne McHugh, because of your commitment to our vision, we don't need to hate on other authors.

To our extended family: brothers, Dennis Perry and Victor Moore, sister, Sherry Moore, godparents, Walter and Marjorie Kimbrough, young nephews, Franklin Perry III, Kadarius Moore, and godsons, Danton Lynn, Dakari Jones, and Dorian Lee, because of your support we have never hated on others with wonderful families since we had our own.

To our assistant Joy Spencer, because you stepped up, we did not have to hate that we would get our project turned in late since you had us on time.

To our friends who mean so much: Jim and Deen Sanders, Antonio and Gloria London, Chett and Lakeba Williams, Bobby and Sarah Lundy, Harry and Torian Colon, Byron and Kim Forest, Donald and Deborah Bradley, because of your endearing friendship, we have no hating going on for people who have close folks in their lives.

To our teens: Dustyn, Sydni, and Sheldyn, because you give us purpose and keep us full, we never hate for a minute we are your parents.

To the media specialists, school administrators, teachers, and educational companies across the country who support us, especially, Veronica Evans from Delaney Educational, because you believed in our work, we were able to connect with Saddleback Educational Publishing on this series and not hate we did not give our all to help readers.

To our new readers, whom we trust will work hard and become successful readers, because you won't give up and won't hate you missed out on being all you want to be.

And to our Savior, whom has allowed us to reap the benefits of our hard work, because You have opened windows for us, we do not hate some doors You have closed for our good.

CHAPTER 1
True Outsider

Amir, where the heck do you think you're going?" my father said angrily. I was just grabbing my keys and heading to work. Dang!

I was a month away from seventeen years old. I loved my pops, for real, but I was sick of him riding me like I was a donkey. I was not an ass. I did what I had to do. I took care of my responsibilities. I had a little side job so I would not have to get spending money from him. Why did he care where I was going? He was a surgeon. He was always gone.

Being a little truthful and a lot sarcastic I said, "What is it now: my room, the dishes, the trash? Done, done, and done. I'm going to work, Dad, that's all."

"Anna, you better do something with this boy because he's getting way too mouthy and trying me way too much."

"Amir, respect your father, honey," my mom said. She never defended me.

I did not hate him, but I wondered what was up his butt because he treated me like dirt. I liked athletics more than academics, and I figured that was his problem. I did not look like him. I did not act like him. I certainly did not think like him. Picture a nerdy black man with glasses, dressed in khakis, a white shirt, and loafers. That was him. I had muscles and swag.

It might have taken me longer than what came to him naturally when it came to the books, but I buckled down and had a 3.75 GPA. So what was his problem? Why was he always riding me? Why did he push me all the time? He wanted my respect, but he had not respected me for most of my life.

Kids I hung around always said they envied what I had—a dad who was a doctor, a dad who was involved in my life, and a dad who lived in my same home. That was just it. The structure I lived in had not much to it. There was some

Sheetrock with some bricks on the outside. However, there certainly was not much love shared on the inside.

As for dreams and goals and stuff that I was supposed to aspire to, I had not really given it much thought. Yeah, I was a junior in high school, and I was almost out of my parents' door. But when I was in middle school, my dad laughed at everything I wanted to be and told me to choose something else. I got tired of trying to come up with something that interested me and that my father didn't think was pointless. He said everything I was looking into did not have an opportunity to bring in six figures. I was a rapper in my elementary school talent show and won. Last time I looked, Jay-Z, Diddy, Kanye West, and other players in the game were holding down big loot. My dad said over his dead body would I get out on stage and make money as a stupid entertainer. Then in the seventh grade, when I got all the awards in football, I wanted to be a professional baller, but of course my father protested. He felt that men banging their heads around was beneath his son's dignity. Then I started looking at more practical jobs, like being a dentist or a veterinarian, but he still thought that paled in comparison to being a surgeon.

I've never been able to measure up. Somewhere between the eighth and ninth grade, I stopped putting myself on his scale. Our relationship was so strained: like a wet paper towel holding a bunch of raw potatoes. Any moment it was going to bust.

"What's going on with you, Amir? You giving me attitude? You're a big boy, but you are not grown. Do I need to remind you of that?" my dad got in my face and asked.

I picked up my left hand to look at my watch, but my dad swatted my hand down real hard. Instinctively, I flexed my muscles and came at him. I was almost six foot one, and he was barely five foot nine. He was the parent, but his body made him look like a kid.

"Honey, just let the boy go on. You're on call tonight, and you might have to go back to the hospital. No stress," my mom said, giving my dad wise advise. "Amir, get on out of here."

"Working at a gym," my dad snorted. "I can get him a job as an orderly at the hospital. At least he'd be around the environment he needs in order to learn something. He needs all the extra help that he can get with his intellect," my dad said, throwing the only jab he could.

I threw my hands up at that moment, walked out the door, and slammed it shut. I did not care if he came out and told me to never come back. It did not matter because for some reason it felt like I did not belong there anyway. What was the good in having a dad who every day made you feel like you were inadequate compared to him? I knew fathers were supposed to have high expectations, but weren't they supposed to love you unconditionally? Goodness gracious, if I would have been born with cerebral palsy or Down syndrome, he would not have been able to take it even though he was a doctor.

When I got to the gym, I was fifteen minutes late. I went to my locker to put up my stuff. I knew I had a class that had already begun, but it was what it was, and I was here now.

"No need to change," said Mr. Wan. He was the small but super strong owner of Cheertowne, the gym where I worked.

"I'm ready, sir. I was just gonna put away my things. I don't have to change, and I'm sorry for being late," I added. Mr. Wan still looked annoyed.

"Sorry is not gonna cut it this time, young man. Head out the door, I don't need you," Mr. Wan said.

Mr. Wan was Asian, and I did not know if he was no nonsense because of his culture, or if he felt the pressure of running a business in a down economy. For years Cheertowne had been known as the gym that trained the best competition squads in the metro Atlanta area, but due to the recession, people could not afford to pay three grand a year for their child to cheer. Many still wanted to come for lessons so when they were finally able to cheer for their school, they would also be able to tumble.

I could get that Mr. Wan had to be tough, but I was not the kind of guy to plead for anything. I was not so cool that I thought I was all that. However, I was not weak either.

"Can I talk to you, sir?" I said in a truly respectful way.

"In my office ... in my office now," he huffed.

Seeing his impatience, I got to the point quickly. "I apologize for being late."

"You have a cell, but you no call. Young people call and text for everything else. You late for work, and you no call," Mr. Wan vented.

Coming clean I said, "Sir, it was my dad."

"Always your dad. Always him not wanting you to be here. He came to my gym angry a couple of times. Maybe you not work here, and Dad won't blow up. I can't let your problem be my problem, Amir. Son, you are growing up, and you must understand you have to handle business."

"You're right, sir," I said to him, owning up to my mistakes.

I knew my dad tripped sometimes. I knew he was home today. I should've planned extra time for him to give me strife.

"But look out your window," I said. We looked through the glass onto the gym floor. "Look at all those little kids. They aren't learning a thing because their favorite coach isn't out there with them. They look bored. They look like they might quit and take their money with them. You need to keep me here. Let me coach. Let me teach. Let me stay."

I guess when he saw what I was talking about he said, "One more time."

I reached out my hand to give him dap, but he didn't know what to do with that.

I couldn't really explain why I liked tumbling. My mom put me in gymnastics after watching the Olympics one year. She felt like I could get a gold medal. My dad approved of the Olympics because it was an elite-type pursuit. I went to the gym, and the tumbling stuff came naturally. To this day, I find it a thrill to help others do spirals and aerials.

Before I could get out there, Lexus, this girl who I used to really kick it with and who worked at the gym, came up to me. "Where have you been?" she whined.

I looked at her like she was insane. What business was it of hers? She was acting way too over the top. It was like she had no life other than me. She'd call me every five minutes, and then she even got a job at the gym to be closer to me. This girl needed to move on.

It started when I met up with her at the movies a few months back. Our hormones started rising, and we made each other feel good. I told her I did not want anything serious, and at first she said she could handle it. But she couldn't. She always wanted more attention from me. I tried breaking up with her three times before school started, but she just wasn't leaving me alone. I wanted to be the one to do the chasing, and I definitely didn't need a girl who wouldn't cut a brother a break.

Thankfully, another co-worker, Carlen, who also went to my high school, saw that I was hemmed up. I gave him a signal. He picked up on it and called me over to my class.

When I walked away, Lexus said, "So it's like that? You just gonna use me up and throw me out with the trash?"

I kept walking. There was no need for me to respond. I definitely did not want her to feel like garbage, but we had no connection. The crazy chick then ran up to me and slapped me hard.

"I'm sorry. I'm sorry. I'm sorry," she cried when I looked at her is a disappointed way.

"These kids in the gym did not see what you did. You better hope Mr. Wan didn't either, or you might lose your job. I was never trying to hurt you, and I never led you on."

She ran out of the gym, and I ran over to the kids. I hoped we stayed in opposite corners because things could only get worse between us.

"Man, these cats ain't gonna go to state," Carlen muttered. We were in the stands waiting for the opening kickoff of the Lockwood Lions. Lexus had tagged along.

"Yeah, 'cause you aren't on the team, right?" I teased and jabbed him lightly on the arm.

"You should be out there," he said, trying to hit me below the belt since he knew I had skills from our days in the little league football.

Carlen got me. I had no words to defend why I was not out there. I was frustrated just being a spectator because I knew I had more athletic ability than most of the boys out on the field. I actually got a little salty with him. I was angry he called me out. Even with a crowded stadium full of packed fans, I wanted to stay to myself.

What was really going on? What was keeping me from going after what I really wanted? Did I really want to play ball?

I noticed Lexus sliding closer and closer to me. I did not want to come to the game with her, but Carlen asked if I'd ride with him, and I said yes, not knowing he told Lexus she could go too. Next thing I knew, her hand was on my thigh. Without thinking, I jumped up like the rest of the crowd and cheered as the Lions entered the field. There was a big man in front of Carlen. He was blocking Carlen's view. I knew if I sat behind him, I would not be able to see the whole field. However, I was a little taller than Carlen, and I'd rather have a bad view than be seated next to crazy Lexus.

"Hey, man," I said, "Wanna switch places? Nobody's in front of me, and you'd have a better view."

"Yeah, man, that'd be great," Carlen said. He quickly switched places.

Lexus huffed. Carlen had binoculars and put them around his neck as he clapped and screamed uncontrollably like he was the Lions number-one fan. I was relieved to have distance between me and the psycho chick, although Carlen's big personality tended to attract a lot of unwanted attention as well.

After Lexus and her pushy ways, I thought the last thing I wanted to be thinking about would be females. But then I saw the cheerleaders out on the field; one girl in particular made me do a double take. I was mesmerized by her glowing chocolate skin, her whipped short haircut, her perfectly proportioned body, and her infectious smile. I yanked Carlen's binoculars away from him. When I looked closer, she was perfect. No fake long hair trying to keep up with the Kardashians. She wasn't all hoochie. Her boobs weren't going to knock you over, but they pulled you in. The girl was beautiful.

When the cheerleaders went over to the sidelines, she was the loudest one. Trying to hype up the crowd, she just made you want to get in the game. I found myself staring.

"Dang, man, did you see that first play?" Carlen shouted, killing my eardrum.

"What happened?" I said, turning my head from the sidelines to the field.

"What you doing, man? Looking at the cheerleaders or something?" he said as he popped the back of my head and took back his binoculars. "All that shiny gold on those girls," Carlen sniffed. "I would have done something more understated," he said, being the fashionable guy that he was.

Lexus sneered, "I know he's not looking at the cheerleaders. They're nothing to look at."

I wanted to remind her that she tried out and didn't make it, but I didn't go there. She was dead wrong anyway. All the girls shaking their pom-poms were the cutest our school had to offer. Of course I had to carry my man card even though Carlen did not, so I played it off like I was into the game.

Turning to Carlen I said, "No, I wasn't looking at the cheerleaders. I just missed the play."

"It's the secondary man, we just got a pick. Dang, they need some help out there. You should go out for the team, Amir. I know you used to play cornerback. Plus, you'd look fine in that uniform."

"Amir used to play football?" Lexus laughed.

As if he was my agent, Carlen replied boldly, "Yeah, he was amazing. This seventh grader just tearing up the field. He was doing his thing." He looked at me. "I don't think you played your eighth-grade year. Did you get hurt or something?"

I just shook my head not wanting to give him a response. The only thing hurt were my feelings when my dad told me I could not suit up again. Thankfully, Carlen's attention went back to the game when the crowd screamed. The more I watched, the more I felt I in the wrong place in the stadium.

When halftime came, the cheerleaders were introduced. Carlen hit me on the leg and said, "Man, you know I don't swing that way, but a few of these girls look good enough to gobble up." I knew they were fine. We both smiled.

"You kidding me?" Lexus muttered. "They are tore up."

"No hating. And you need my binoculars. The juniors on varsity are hotter than one hundred degrees," Carlen said, fanning himself.

The cheerleaders were tumbling, and I was impressed. However, when the announcer got to the last girl—the one I'd been eyeing all first half—she could not do anything. Maybe she could do it, but she froze up. Whatever it was, she ran off the field.

I dashed out of the stands before my two co-workers could ask me anything. I was going really fast through the crowd, not knowing why I was looking for her, but her exact image would not leave my brain. I came to a complete stop when I got to the concession stand. What I saw first were her legs. Beautiful.

She was at the back of the line and I stood behind her. I was moved, as I could hear her weeping. I didn't know this girl, but I wanted to dry her every tear. I was a semi-pro at teaching folks how to tumble. I was known for helping girls with mental blocks break free and fly. If helping her acquire the skills to be competitive would put a smile back on her face, I had to let her know the man standing behind her could help. Without thinking, I touched her arm and said some encouraging words. I had to let her know I was serious. She could do this. I made her blush, and that made me feel good.

Before we could carry on a conversation, an annoying voice yelled out, "Amir, why'd you leave me?"

My boiling point dropped to a new low. Before the cheerleader could notice, I dealt with the problem. I dashed out of line and ushered Lexus away from the crowd.

She went off right away. "I want be with you. I want to show you how much I care. I know I was a little forceful the other day with the slap and all, but being too sweet was annoying. I wanted you to see that I had a little fire in me too. I can show you right now how hot I am," Lexus said.

At that moment I wanted to yell out, "Is there anybody who wants to get lucky? There's a girl right here willing to give it up."

Dang, the last thing I wanted her to do was think we were together. As we walked back to our seats in the bleachers, I kept repeating to her over and over that she wasn't my girl. But it seemed my words were going in one ear and out the other.

"I mean, what do you want me to do, Lexus?" I did not spare her the harsh words. "I've ignored you. I've tried being friends ..."

Tears were shed. I felt bad. I wasn't going to back down though. There was really no hope, and she needed to get that. I threw up my hands and sat on the other side of Carlen.

When the game was over, the Lions were victors. Despite a bad defense, we found a way to hold on. Our quarterback, Blake Strong, had an arm that was the difference maker.

I was really bummed out that I did not drive. I had no idea that Carlen was going to be hanging out at the post-game party. He loved talking about fashion and the cheerleaders' showy uniforms. I just rolled my eyes. However, when I got into the party and saw the mystery cheerleader walking in with her crew, I wasn't in such a rush to jet.

"You never look at me like that," Lexus blurted out, startling me. "You're putting me down for a Cheerio?"

"What's that?" I said, looking at her truly confused.

Educating me she said, "It's what the show *Glee* calls their cheerleaders."

"I don't watch *Glee*," I snapped. I wanted to get away. Fast. "I don't really watch any TV," I said more slowly, trying to sound less rude.

"Well, you should because it's about people who feel out of place and are not in the in crowd," Lexus said. "You see all those ballers over there, guys who won the game in the last minute. Well, you're standing over here with me. Those girls that you're eyeing so hard and think have it going on won't give you the time of day because you don't have a letterman's jacket. I'm not a nerd or a nobody. But to them, I don't exist. Neither do you. So why you think you're all that and deserve one of their girls, I haven't the foggiest. Those guys will chew you up and spit you out."

I just threw up my hands and walked over to the mystery girl. One of her girlfriends was standing there. They both smiled my way.

The friend said, "Hi, I'm Charli Black, and this is my girlfriend, Hallie Ray."

"It's you," Hallie said. Then she hugged me real tight.

At that moment, I was conscious of all the football players eyeing me like I had stepped on their turf. But whatever. They weren't the only ones that had game. Hallie Ray was lovely, and I could tell from the way she was feeling me that I wasn't a true outsider. To her I had something.

We finally got back to Cheertowne, and I retrieved my car. Lexus pouted all the way back, and I was thrilled when she left me alone. I was also glad Carlen had a key to the gym because I had to use the bathroom. Carlen startled me as he had to go too.

"Boy, you better let someone know you coming in here," I called out, finishing my business.

I didn't feel uncomfortable using the bathroom with a guy like Carlen, but I was jumpy tonight.

"Man, who else would you think it was?" Carlen asked.

"Crazy Lexus," I replied quickly. I went to wash my hands.

"Yeah, I don't know what you gonna do with that girl," Carlen said. "All she talks about is you. If you don't take her back, I don't know what she'll do to herself."

"Dude, don't joke," I replied. I really felt she was unstable. "Look, my curfew is one and it's one now. I'm out. You ready to lock up?"

Carlen hurried and washed his hands. "Yeah, I gotta take Lexus home."

I joked, "And talk some sense into her. Dang."

Walking to the front door of the gym, Carlen said, "I'm not gonna talk too much sense into her, or she'll try to talk to me. That needs to be your headache 'cause ain't no telling what that girl is willing to do to keep you."

When we went outside, I saw Lexus sitting on the curb, sobbing. I wanted to just keep going and pretend I didn't see her there, but she cried louder when she saw me.

"Lexus, what are you crying for?" I asked though I was truly not interested.

Lexus whined, "Like you even tryna ask. I saw you tonight talking to that cheerleader. Is it because she's so popular? Are you so superficial and caught up in all of that?"

I didn't even know Hallie Ray and certainly didn't know if anything would come of the feeling I had for her. Suddenly, Lexus jumped up and started beating on my chest. Enough was enough, and I grabbed her wrists tightly.

"Stop this," I said to her. "Carlen, get your girl."

Lexus shouted, "Then love me!"

Before I could respond, she was in my arms and slobbering all over my face.

"I gotta go," I said. I tried to pull the girl off but she was stuck to me like a spider's web. She would not let me be. She held on to my shirt. Thankfully, Carlen came over. He stepped between us, but she still held on.

"Lexus, girl, dang! What's up? You don't want him to have to call the police, do you, girl? You're starting to act like a stalker," Carlen tried rationalizing. "Girlfriend, get a grip."

Finally, she loosened her hold enough for me to completely pull away. Steamed, I went over to my new Mustang. I looked down, and noticed the driver's side front tire was flat. I knew I was going to be in for it because it was already one fifteen. Thankfully I had a spare in the back of my car. Problem was the back driver's side tire was flat too. Just then I threw down my keys, rushed over to Lexus, and pushed her.

I shouted, "What the heck did you do to my car?"

She gave me this grim smile. This girl was acting crazy. Now I really did want to call the police.

"Oh snap," Carlen called out when he saw my car. "Girl, did you really do that?"

Not answering the question, Lexus announced, "Take me home. I don't have a knife on me. However, I told you, you'd regret it if you didn't come back to me."

"So now you're threatening me?" I said to her. "Could you help me with this tire and then get her outta my face, Carlen?"

Carlen and I both had Mustangs. His was not new, but his spare would fit. He told me I could use it. It was good having his help putting them on, all the while seething that the person who did this was just a few feet away.

"I told you she was wild," Carlen said while Lexus was seated in his car. "I didn't know she was capable of doing all this though. I don't even wanna take her home. What if she thinks I'm you and slits my throat? She's gotta have some kind of box cutter or something."

"At least I'll be able to tell the police who did it," I teased him.

"Oh, so you think you got jokes?"

"Now you see, ain't nothing funny about Lexus. I can't believe she did this," I fumed.

Like a girl in a horror movie who pops up out of nowhere, she hovered over the both of us and screamed, "Prove it!"

Carlen squealed like a little girl. I stood up. My patience with her was gone.

"Get back over to the car, Lexus," I demanded.

I knew she was upset. I knew she was mad. I knew she was ticked that I ended things, but for real, she was taking things too far. Yeah, my loving might be all that, but truth be told, if she hadn't shown me she was crazy, I might've broke her off a little piece sometime before she gradu-ated. Now all that was over. If she came near me again, no telling what I'd do.

So I stood my ground and demanded, "Get to Carlen's car."

That scared her because she left. When I got home it was 1:50 a.m. The lights in my house were on, and my parents were sitting on the couch.

"Dad, I'm sorry. I know my curfew is one, but somebody slashed my tires," I tried explaining.

He squinted. "Someone slashed your tires? Where was this?"

"At the gym."

"I told you working down there wasn't the best environment. By working in the hood, my son has enemies. You need to be doing something more productive and working someplace safer. People going nowhere are always jealous. You need to be better than that and not care what the little man thinks. Your brother is home from college. Anthony Jr. won that national science competition. He's been waiting since eleven to tell you about it. We were going to celebrate, cake and all. You only said you were going to the game, and even in the worst case your curfew was at one."

"I rode with some co-workers to the game, and I left my car. I didn't know they were going to the dance."

"Do they trump your parents? Do they make your decisions? I don't even care who they are. You could've let us know something. You have a cell phone."

"Son, I was worried," my mom added. The mood was getting ugly.

I looked in her eyes and could tell she was weary from hearing my dad go on and on. I hated that she always had to defend me. When was he going to cut me slack?

"Okay, Dad, what do you want me to say? I was irresponsible. I'm sorry I didn't call. But I fixed the tires on my own. I didn't call you to take care of them for me."

"Your tires aren't fixed," he said. "You have spares on. But you're right, the job is yours to have them fixed. I bought you a new car. Upkeep is your responsibility. Your little job can pay for new tires. I'm not gonna give you a dime to take care of any of that. And as soon as you make enough money to do that, you're gonna quit."

"I'm not quitting my job," I said defiantly.

"You're gonna do exactly what I say," my dad snarled. "Some young men grow up and handle their responsibilities. Other young men just want to try adults. Newsflash for you, son. Nothing around here is your own. You do it my way, or you can get stepping. Why can't you be like Anthony?"

"Because I'm Amir."

"Right, the son who doesn't measure up to my expectations. Just looking at you makes me sick," my dad said before storming away.

I knew that was how he felt, but he never blatantly came out and said as much. Hearing that solidified the fact that as soon as I graduated from high school, I was not coming back to this house. Though I was his son, he certainly didn't act like my father. He told me in no uncertain terms that I was a true outsider.

CHAPTER 2

Opportunity Knocks

I'm getting the heck out of here, Anthony," I said to my brother when he appeared in my doorway. I was done, so I went to my room and immediately started packing my things.

"Mom's talking to Dad right now. You know he has high standards, and he didn't really mean any of that. Don't let him get to you, bro," Anthony said.

I vented, "Come on, man, don't try that stuff with me. He's always on my case. He *never* says those things to you."

"Mom is calming him down now. I don't know what's going on with him."

"Exactly, so why should I stay here and take it? Am I lying, Anthony? Is what I'm saying not true?" I asked. I wanted my brother to admit our dad treated me unfairly.

I looked at my brother. He was a distinguished and smart-looking guy. He wasn't a nerd because he had swag. There was something about him that exuded confidence. You just knew that he was destined to be the next doctor in the family. My father was angry that I didn't have what he saw in Anthony. Honestly, I used to detest my brother because I was always treated like the stepchild. Anthony and I were tight now. When I was through packing my bags, my brother stood in my way and wouldn't move.

"Come on, man. Don't make me hurt you," I said, looking at the skinnier version of myself and knowing that it would not take much energy for me to have him get out of my way.

"Amir, you are not going to hurt me. I'm trying to help. I love you, bro. You know Dad is over the top sometimes. You just don't hear him going off on me. That doesn't mean he doesn't do it."

"Anthony, don't lie to my face," I said to my brother. I knew that in our dad's eyes, Anthony could do no wrong.

My big brother would still not let me by. "I'm not letting you out of the door, Amir."

"Anthony, move!"

"No! Bro, where are you going to go?" my brother said. He made a grab for my bag.

"What difference does it make? I'ma be far away from here." I shook my head.

When I was not looking, my brother reached for my arm. On impulse, I tugged it away real hard, and he flew back into the door. It made quite a bit of noise, and he bumped his head.

"Dang, Anthony! You all right?" I said in a panic.

It took no time for our parents to come bursting in my room.

"What's going on in here?" my father said. When he saw my brother down on the ground holding his head, he looked over at me and grabbed my shirt collar.

Immediately my brother stood up and got in between us and said, "Dad, I fell."

My father responded to Anthony, "Oh, because if your brother hit you, I—"

"What, Dad?!" I said angrily as I hit my chest. "What? If I would've hit him … what?"

"Amir, calm down!" Anthony said, trying to be a peacemaker.

It was becoming abundantly clear that my father had something against me. I could not live my life to please him anymore. I could not allow him to dictate my happiness or my anger.

"I'm out of here, Pops," I said. I grabbed my bag and started to walk away.

My dad yelled, "If you leave now, you are not coming back. You don't get to dictate. You're not grown, boy. Just because you don't like what I have to say, you think you can leave? I'm the parent. That's what's wrong with you. You're tough in the wrong places, always letting your anger get the best of you. Take what I have to say like a man and be better for it. Don't try to run from your problems!"

"Don't scream, honey," my mom said. "Talk to him. *Please*, he can't leave."

When she started crying, I turned back and said, "Mom, I don't want you to be upset. I'm going to be okay."

"You can't leave, honey. You and your dad are going to work this out."

"Do not speak for me, Anna," my father hissed. With one look and touch from my mother, I guess my dad had a change of heart because he got real calm. "Look, son," he said in a milder tone. "I'm not trying to get your mom all worked up. I've got to go to the hospital. You stay here and calm your mom down. We'll talk about this later."

His calm demeanor was crazy. When I did not think there was any way things would work out, my dad just changed. It was like he was two different people, like Dr. Jekyll and Mr. Hyde or something. Thankfully, Mr. Hyde was gone. My mom calmed down, and my brother was not seriously hurt.

I was able to chill, but not for long. Someone was banging on our front door. It was bizarre since it was after two thirty in the morning. When I answered the door, it was Lexus.

"What are you doing here?" I growled.

"I had to make sure you were okay. Someone slashed your tires. I know you thought it was me, but—"

"Lexus, please. It's best we don't even talk," I said, knowing that the chick standing in front of me was full of it.

"Is there anybody home?" Lexus said as she tried to invite herself into my house.

Our bodies were practically rubbing up against each other. Knowing that this chick was crazier than my dad, I really did not know what to do. She was hitting me, vandalizing my property, crying uncontrollably. She just did not seem stable.

"Lexus, seriously? I'm going to have to ask you to leave," I demanded, putting my hand in between our bodies.

Suddenly, she grabbed my hand and put it on her left breast. "You like the feel of that, huh?"

"Okay, all right, Mom?" I yelled out. I had no other option.

She backed up. "Your mother's here?"

"Yeah, my mom is here. It's two thirty in the morning. Where else would she be?"

"I don't see her coming," she said, trying to nuzzle my neck.

"Mom!" I yelled with more urgency.

"See, no one's coming," she looked around and said. "Why are you making this so difficult, Amir? I want to be with you. I want to make you feel good like I did before. Like if we reconnect, you won't push me away, and I won't have to show you what you're missing and make you regret leaving me. You understand what I'm saying?"

"Are you saying you slashed my tires?"

She took her hand and grabbed right between my legs. I wanted to punch her. For real, she was loony.

"Mom!" I shouted as loud as I could after stepping back.

Finally my mom came from around the corner. "What is going on? It's the middle of the night. Hello, young lady. Can I help you?"

"Mom, she needs to go. I've asked her to leave and she won't."

"Oh," my mom said, clearly taken aback.

"Why would you treat me like this? You invite me over and then you tell me to leave. I want to meet your mom. I want her to know that I'm a wonderful young lady," Lexus said, trying to hold in her tears, which I presumed to be completely fake.

"What's going on here, Amir?" my mom said. I knew that my mom must be anxious to know what was going on.

"Let me introduce myself. I'm Lexus Stanley. I'm Amir's girlfriend."

My ears were popping from the high pitch of the tale she told. I started choking at that moment. My mom hit my back.

"Amir, are you okay?" my mother asked.

Clearing my throat I said, "What is this? I can't believe you're telling my mom that you're my girlfriend."

"Well, I was until you broke up with me last week," Lexus blurted out.

"If my son is saying that you're not his girlfriend, sweetheart, I'm sure you respect that," my mom said, thinking Lexus was a rational girl with self-respect.

"Yes, ma'am, but actions speak louder than words," Lexus said, as she looked at my mom and insinuated that we had been physical.

"Okay, that's enough. See you later. Thank you so much. Amir can't have any company. It's the middle of the night. Your parents must be worried about you," my mom said with a thin smile. "You need to go home now. Thank you, dear."

My mom kept walking forward, and Lexus had to back up. When Lexus was out the door, my mom shut it and looked at me. She was not happy, and neither was I.

"This is the kind of foolishness your dad was talking about. You open up your pants, think you're grown, get with any little girl, and you find somebody who's crazy. She could be trying to get pregnant. I hope you used something."

"Yeah, Mom, I did, dang. I don't want to talk about this."

"Well, obviously we are going to have to talk about this because the young lady—and I *do* use the term loosely—who just left here was irrational."

"I know, Mom. I know she's the one who slashed my tires. She slapped me. She shows up at my house saying she's my girl. I don't know what to do. I ended it, but she won't accept it."

"If it continues, we're going to go to her house and talk to her parents. Just keep your distance from her and learn from this. Don't get involved with any girl until you get to know more about her. I hope you see every opportunity isn't a door you should open."

I woke up to a knife at my throat, a gun to my head, and a rope around my neck. Thankfully it was just a nightmare, but Lexus had me all messed up. She had seeped into my dreams. From the quiet in the house I guessed that my dad was still on duty at the hospital and my mom had gone by herself to the Saturday church service. After the drama of last night, it was nice of her to let me sleep in. But then I smelled breakfast cooking. Who was in the house?

"You can't let these chicks keep you up," Anthony said as he scrambled some eggs.

He winked, as he saw I was surprised he was cooking. College obviously served him well. He also was in sync with me. He knew exactly what I had been going through in the last six hours.

"How'd you know I could not sleep?"

"Man, I came in there one time and you were screaming. Mom came in my room earlier and told me what happened with the girl earlier today. Chicks can sometimes be crazy."

"I don't know what to do. I told her we were through."

"That's why I tell brothers all the time at school … everything that glitters is not gold. We get caught up in the bodies, the pretty faces, and letting what's between our legs dictate—"

"Should've told me that," I said, grabbing the plate to eat some of his French toast.

"Well, from now on remember if she's showing herself crazy and won't take no for an answer, I don't care if she's nice and pretty, leave her alone because she's foolish," my brother said.

I nodded. "So what can I do now?"

We sat to eat, and he said, "When I have girls who are really stalker types, I date somebody else. I've found that somewhere in their warped little minds, when they see you're still single, they think you're holding out for them. When they see you with somebody else, nine times out of ten, they'll move on. But if you got one of those one out of ten who are insane, ain't nothing really that you can do except call the police if it gets more physical. Slashing tires today, slashing body parts tomorrow. And that ain't cool. Speaking of which, go ahead and eat up. Mom said she wants me to take you by the tire place."

Normally, I'd have eaten a lot more of my brother's tasty French toast, but I couldn't get my mind off of Lexus and her unstable behavior. I hoped she would get herself under control. For sure, I was going to be staying away.

My brother saw me deep in thought. "But you probably ain't looking for nobody else right about now. You probably want a break from women, huh?"

A big smile came across my face.

"Oh snap, tell me about this one. What's up?"

"It's nothing."

"Oh yeah, it's something. You can't even hold in your excitement, but tell me you have learned and researched this new girl."

I bowed my head. "Not really."

"So you ain't learned anything?"

"Well, I haven't hit it yet, that's for sure."

"Okay, that's good. Don't go there until you're sure."

"That's the thing, that's not even why I like her. I mean, I'm definitely attracted to her, but I don't know … there's something about her. She's beautiful. She's outgoing, and she's like no other girl I've ever met. I saw her cheering at the game, and I didn't want to take my eyes off of her."

"Did you introduce yourself? Come on, I know you got game, what's up?" my brother said, stunning me that he was cooler than I realized.

"You know I got game, huh?" I laughed. "I started talking to her but I had to walk away because the psycho was calling me." What you doing over in school? I thought you had your head way stuck in the books so that you didn't know what a girl was," I said, putting him in a head lock.

"Oh, I study, little brother, but there's a lot more to college than books. Now you? Stressed about Dad, freaked out over a stalker chick, and now you think you can tackle me because you've got a few more muscles. Don't forget I know karate," Anthony said as he elbowed me in the gut.

When I keeled over, he kicked me in the chest and made me fall to one knee.

"All right, you got me. You got me."

"That's what I thought," Anthony teased before we hugged.

When I got to the gym, I wanted to call in sick because I saw Lexus's car. If she was in there, then that was the last place I wanted to be. However, I knew I got in trouble last time for being late. If I was a no-show, I probably would not have a job. And at this point, I really needed it because I was going to have to pay for new tires. Though my mom bought them, I knew my Dad would be making sure that I paid her back.

Thankfully, I had a job that could give me dollars. I stumbled into teaching tumbling. It was actually a stress-free job. I was dealing with little girls who usually whined because they were scared to trust their training to flip. When I worked with them, I had a knack for getting them to loosen up and enjoy it. Before they knew it, they were doing so much more than they thought they could. I called it flying.

As soon as I walked in the gym, a crowd of over fifty girls ran my way like I was Santa Claus. Then I saw a beautiful sight. Hallie Ray from Friday was there. I smiled on the inside, knowing she had taken my advice to come to the gym to learn how to tumble. How cool was that?

Lexus was her instructor, but all the noise made her look my way. When our eyes met, it was like Hallie was asking to be rescued. She did not have to say any more. I knew what was up. Without even having to manipulate a way to change places with her, our boss called Lexus into his office, and he yelled for me to teach our new student.

"Hey, you," I said to her.

"I didn't know what happened. You had me come here to learn how to tumble, and you weren't even here. What's up with that?"

"You should've called me and let me know you were coming."

"You never gave me your number," she said, batting her eyelashes at me. She had such warm, friendly eyes.

"Well, let's fix that right now."

We both reached for our phones, but neither of us had them. It was just natural for teens to have a cell glued to our hips. We both laughed, remembering the cells were in the locker rooms.

With frustration Hallie said, "Amir, I've been working on this for about thirty minutes with Lexus, but I can't do this."

"Oh no you don't," I said and put my hands on her shoulders. "None of that talk in my gym. The word can't is not allowed here."

"And what are you going to do if I say that word again? Spank me?" she teased.

"I don't think you want to try me." I smiled, unable to hide the fact that I was digging this girl.

She allowed me to help her tumble. Somehow we fell and I ended up on top. Not trying to be presumptuous but it seemed she liked our position. As she could not stop smiling, I knew the door was definitely open for the two of us. I was for sure going to explore the chance.

"Hey, guy, what's up? I'm Brenton," this guy on the football team introduced himself to me during gym class. "You're Amir Knight. We had PE together last year. You can flat out run. We also played little league football years ago."

"Hey yeah. What's up, man?" I said as we slapped hands.

"Do you have Coach Strong or Coach Woods?" Brenton asked, carrying on our conversation.

Skeptical but cool, I said, "I'm in Coach Strong's class."

"Yeah, me too. From what I hear, we're going to be playing flag football," Brenton said as if this was right up his alley.

"Coach Strong is your uncle, right?" I asked Brenton, remembering he had clout with the in crowd.

"Yeah, he's my mother's brother. We're supposed to be competing even though it's just a PE class. My uncle thinks you should give one hundred percent. He's a diehard coach—*x*'s and *o*'s are all that's in his blood. He even wants the girls to hit hard and it's flag football," Brenton said while looking at Coach Strong.

We both laughed. I wasn't a loner, but I did not hang out with popular kids or feel the need to make myself be in the in crowd. However, I found it interesting that Brenton initiated a conversation with me, and he wasn't hanging out with some of the loudmouthed football players a few feet away talking trash.

"I'm gonna pick you for my team," Brenton said, seeing his teammates were strategizing. "We're going to kill 'em."

Someone tapped my shoulder and when I turned around, I felt like I swallowed a weight. Figuratively, I sunk to the ground. I did not even want to say hello. I knew I could not be rude. However, I did not want to get Lexus started because I did not know which Lexus had shown up to greet me.

"Yes?" I said in the calmest voice I could muster up.

"I just came here to tell you that the little cheerleader girl you like—"

"Okay, hold up, Lexus. Just mind your own business."

Brenton squinted and said, "Oh, sounds like somebody's jealous."

Lexus barked, "I'm not even talking to you, dumb jock."

"I'll catch up to you in a minute," Brenton said to me and walked away.

"You wanted to tell me something?" I asked.

"Your girl, she was in the locker room talking about you," Lexus said sarcastically.

I found it hard to believe what she was saying so I asked, "Hallie was confiding in you?"

"I overheard it. Look, there's no need to get an attitude with me, Amir. I'm trying to help you. You're the best tumbling coach in the whole gym, yet you fell on top of her while you were teaching her yesterday. I saw the way y'all's eyes were glued to each other. Before you get your heart broken, I just want you to know what she really thinks about you."

The whole conversation was ironic. I could not even sleep the other night when Lexus filled my brain with nightmares. But I slept like a baby the next night because the moment with Hallie when we were in each other's arms messed me up in a good way.

Lexus continued, "Basically, her friends told her that you were nobody. You're not in any sports, and nobody knows who you are. Since they're so high on themselves, they told her that she's too good to talk to someone with no stats."

I saw Hallie coming into the gym. She looked more beautiful then I remembered. Only difference was she had a worried look on her face, and she was headed my way. Lexus looked like she wanted to claw Hallie's eyes out. I was not going to let that go down.

"If you don't believe me, ask her yourself," Lexus said, and she stormed off.

The two of them exchanged some words I couldn't hear. Hallie's frown deepened. Then she came by me.

"Please, don't believe anything she just said. She took everything she heard out of context. She cornered me in the bathroom and basically told me that I'm not good enough to have any interest in you."

"Just so you know …," I said. "I don't let people influence my decisions, and I give people the benefit of the doubt. So we're good. When you're dealing with people, they always reveal their true selves." I gave Hallie a squeeze on her shoulder.

"I don't understand. What are you saying? Are you waiting for me to put my foot in my mouth?"

"Nah, you're reading too much into it. What I'm saying is I mean it's all good until you show me otherwise, unless you tell me right now you gonna break my heart," I said playfully, stroking her chin.

She started blushing but did not get a chance to respond, because Coach Strong called us all outside to begin flag football. Brenton was right. He was a drill sergeant. All of this was *way* serious to him. I was on Brenton's team, and I did not want to just do well so I could get a good grade. I wanted to shut down the other football players who were talking all that junk. Brenton thought that together we could show them. I was up for the challenge and we did just that. On offense when he threw the ball to me, I scored. On defense when the ball was thrown to a receiver I was guarding, I intercepted it. When it was thrown to the girls, I intercepted it. I had a good time doing my thing, and I didn't even realize anyone else had noticed until Coach Strong called my name to come over to the sidelines and talk to him.

"Are you a junior, young man?" Coach asked.

"Yes, sir. I'm a junior."

Impressed with me, he said, "Why aren't you on my football field? You're killing them."

"It's just a bunch of girls, sir, and guys who do more talking than playing. It's easy to run circles around them. I'm not doing anything special."

"Well, I've been a football coach for a long time. Let me be the judge of what's special. You've got unique skills. Your ability to jump vertically is impressive. You're not a short guy, but it's like you double your size when you jump in the air. It's crazy. And your hands—nice and big—ready to grab the ball. I don't normally do this, but I would really like for you to come out and be a part of my team. I've got some holes in the secondary."

"You sure do," I said, not thinking who I was talking to.

Not mad that I stated the obvious, he asked, "You've seen the team play?"

"I went to the first game Friday, but I missed the scrimmage. The guy on the right corner, I don't know if he just has nerves, but he's not going after the ball. Your opponent picked up on it and just kept throwing the ball to the receiver he was defending. He didn't have poor coverage; he had no courage."

"So you're saying you can do a better job?" Coach Strong asked.

I just threw my hands up. "I'm not saying that."

"Well, it sounds like that's exactly what you're saying. What do you say? Can you stay after school for practice today? What's your parents' numbers? Who do I need to call to make this happen? I need you on my team."

Maybe I was scared. Scared to go after something that I was gifted at because I knew it would be a battle at my house. Or maybe I was scared because I knew I was good once, but maybe I wasn't good anymore. What was going on with me? I knew I couldn't be on his team.

So I said, "Thanks for the offer, Coach, but I'm not interested."

"Well, I'm going to pretend I didn't hear that just now, and I'll let you think about it. I'll see you next time this class meets, and I will ask you again," Coach said. "You've got swag, guts, and ability. I'm giving you an opportunity to put that where it belongs. Possible scholarship for sure if I coach you. You can't close the door when opportunity knocks."

CHAPTER 3

Yes, Man

I lay in my bed and reflected on the fact that the last week had been a blast. That was not because I had no run-ins with my father. It was not because I was doing really well in school. It was not because in the football unit in PE I was still soaring. Though all three things were true, what had really made my week dynamic was that after school I was at the gym and Hallie came for lessons. Our time together was marvelous.

One day she brought me a card that read, "Thanks for believing in me." Another time she brought me a smoothie and said it was a thank you because I made her have energy, and she wanted to pour some back into me. She also smiled and thanked me every time I assisted her with a flip. I liked everything about her: her walk, her talk, her smile, and her conversation. Her very being got me excited.

I knew I needed to ask her out. When she had tumbling success, it was the perfect time to want to take her some place to celebrate. Thankfully, she said yes.

"What's up, little brother?" Anthony asked, coming into my room and turning on the lights.

"I'm tryna get some sleep, man," I replied.

"Please. I hear you in here wrestling. That crazy girl still tripping?"

"I don't even know how to describe *her*," I said to my brother as I sat up.

It was good that he went to Georgia Tech, because on the weekends he'd come home and hang. He was now a sophomore in college, but we talked way more now than we ever did when we both went to Lockwood High.

Frowning to show he hated I still had stalker drama, he said, "What is she doing?"

"Every day last week I got some kinda love note or something in my locker."

"She has your combination?"

"Nah, boy," I said, letting him know I wasn't loony too. "She stuck the note through the little slats. She is wild."

"So have you taken my advice? Have you showed her you moved on?"

Shrugging I said, "I think she gets it."

"What you mean?"

"There's this girl named Hallie."

"The cheerleader you were talking about. Okay," my brother said, smiling.

"I took her out today," I said.

"Where'd you take her, big spender?"

"You know Dad ain't breaking me off any money, so we went to McDonald's."

"Okay, I'm sure she loved that," Anthony teased.

"Yeah, whatever, I think we had a real good time. We did argue though."

"Oh, share it," my brother said.

"She called me a punk."

My brother looked confused. I reached out and gave him dap. We were on the same page.

"As much swag as I got? Exactly," I said.

"No, I like this girl, she's not tryna inflate that brain of yours," my brother said, swatting me with his jacket. "Spill it, Amir, why'd she call you a punk, man?"

Still amazed at how different my brother had become, I asked, "How'd you get so cool all of a sudden?"

"Don't avoid the question. Why'd she call you a punk?"

"She wants me to play football."

"You gave that up a long time ago."

"Maybe I shouldn't have," I answered. There, I said it. I was wrestling with the idea of playing.

My brother taunted, "What? You can't play."

"Forget it," I said, noticing my brother thought the whole talk of me playing football was a joke.

"Why you getting upset?"

"Because you and Dad kill me, man. It's like if I'm not into science or engineering then my dreams and goals don't matter."

"Hey, I'm just saying you gave up football. I didn't know it was a dream or goal of yours. I don't want you to be holding on to something that you're too late for. I mean, the season has already started anyway. You're a junior; your high school days are almost over. What am I not getting here?"

"Dude, in PE class my teacher is Coach Strong, the football coach. He saw me playing in some games during class ..."

"Wait, the same skills you had way back in little league football, you can still do?" Anthony said in an impressed tone.

"Yeah, man, I was catching balls left and right. I really like defense. My speed is there. Those tall receivers think they got me, but I leap up and snatch the ball from them. I don't know."

"And?" Anthony asked.

"And he asked me to play for the team."

Needing clarity my brother asked, "Even though the season has started?"

"Yeah, we're real messed up in the secondary right now. We got a shot at the state title, but if he doesn't fix the problem with the DBs, he's gonna get burned game after game. That's why Hallie and I had it out; I told him no."

"But clearly I see you wanted to say yes," Anthony said, getting right to it.

"She got mad at me when I told her I did not want to play, and when she stormed off, it was so cute. I followed her, and the next thing I know we were kissing."

"That's good, right?"

"Well, then she got all upset. She can't kiss," I said, trying not to laugh as I remembered the event.

"Oh snap," my brother laughed.

"Right. Then she started crying on me, and I thought oh no, not another Lexus."

"She ain't crazy too, is she?" Anthony asked.

"Nah, it was deeper than that. I thought I had problems with Dad, but she's got worse problems at home. And don't go telling Dad or nothing either," I said, remembering my brother used to be my dad's DVR.

"Tell him what?"

"What I'm about to say—that I like this girl whose mom is on drugs."

Anthony shook his head. "Oh, Amir, I don't know if you wanna get messed up with that."

"She can't help what her mom is. The lady doesn't even live there. Her dad forbids her to see her mom anyway. It's a mess."

"Dang, I feel bad for her."

"Yeah," I said. "Then I think when we got back to the gym, Lexus saw we were connecting."

"Well, that's good, right? You can get the crazy girl off your back. Now all you gotta do is handle a highly emotional one. You ready?"

"I can't explain it, but yeah."

"Well, forget the girls for a sec and let me clear up something. If you wanna play football, I think you need to go for it."

"But Dad ..."

"But Dad what?" Anthony asked. "Dad has to live his own life. He can't live yours. You shouldn't have to sneak around to do something you think he doesn't want you to do. You need to talk to him."

I gave my brother a look. "Actions speak louder than words. Do you really think he loves me?"

My brother said, "Yes, he loves you, Amir, and if being out there on the football field is what you want to do, talk to him about it. I trust that he's going to say yes. My brother, a baller ... I can see that because you were bad back in the day. Go for it."

When he turned off my light and walked out of my room, I was happy I had a big brother who cared enough to listen to what was going on in my world. His advice was sound. As much as I wanted to think that I did not care about football, I knew it was in my blood. At least I deserved to give myself the chance to see if the skills I believed were still in me were truly there. Coach told me to think it over, so why not give it a try?

"Amir Knight, what brings you to my office?" Coach Strong said in a voice I could not make out as either happy or indifferent.

"I came to see about playing ball for you, Coach."

As he took his arm and balled fist and pulled it down in the air, Coach Strong yelled, "Yes!"

His excitement was so loud that the commotion going on in the locker room ceased. I felt all eyes looking at me. He had a comfortable-looking couch in his office with two blankets. I did not know whether to curl under those and hide or face the challenge.

"I watched you in PE. Your conditioning is better than some of my players. My nephew Brenton is the captain of defense. I'm going to pair you up with him. All you have to do is pick up the playbook and learn our three-four scheme," he said, showing me the book. "Also, there's some paperwork that you will have to have your folks fill out. But for now, let's go practice. Do you have cleats, pads, anything?" Coach asked me.

I shook my head. He invited me to this party. He was going to have to make sure I had all that I needed to participate. The gift I brought was my talent. I could only hope it would not fail me.

"All right, let me get with the equipment manager and introduce you to our defensive coordinator. Coach Grey, will you step into my office?" Coach Strong called out. I could feel all eyes on me.

I had thick skin, so comments here and there did not mean anything to me. I did not come out here to make friends. I came out here to play. An older Caucasian gentlemen came into Coach Strong's office, touched my shoulders, and pushed them back. He sized me up from head to toe and gave Coach Strong a thumbs-up.

"I saw you playing in class a couple days ago," Coach Grey said with a smile.

"You did?" I asked.

"Yeah, Coach called me out of history to watch you. We've been nervous though. We did not think you'd come out. We'll really see if you got some guts. You were playing with babies in PE class. On my defensive team, you're playing with men. Some teams we go up against are bar-barians. However, just because you showed up, I think you might be able to cut it."

"I appreciate that, Coach. I will work hard for you," I said, knowing I'd give my all.

"Yeah, and you got a knack for the ball," Coach Grey said.

In every drill they did, the team was lacking in my opinion. I knew they had gone through summer workouts, camp, a scrimmage, and one game. I had what was called fresh legs because I had not been grinding with them day in and day out. However, to me they had no heart.

"Why you gotta come out here and make us look bad?" a tall defensive end said. He stood almost six feet four inches and weighed around two forty.

"Don't let Leo get to you," Brenton from PE class said.

I nodded. "I'm just out here doing my thing. Not trying to cause problems."

I wanted to tell that Leo dude that he needed to step it up if he had a problem with what I was doing. Again, I came to play. I was rusty and needed to give one hundred percent if I was going to do this.

"That's what we need, some new blood out here to push us all. I'm glad you're joining the team," Brenton said.

"I'm just trying it out today."

"Well, I'm glad you're trying it out," Brenton said. He stretched out his hand for me to give him dap.

"Why don't y'all just go ahead and kiss," Wax, the snobby senior who thought he was all that, teased.

I shook Brenton's hand, ignoring the jab. When we lined up to run a few plays, our quarterback threw a deep pass for Wax to catch. I stepped in front of him. I shut him up with my actions.

And Brenton teased back, "Kiss the ball good-bye."

I took the pigskin to the end zone for a TD. I was not nearly as big as Leo, but I didn't mind putting hits on running backs and quarterbacks either. Basically, wherever the ball was, that's where I was trying to be. There were a few long passes thrown, and that's when I was able to show my speed. I went one on one against our best receiver, Landon King. He was also a junior. He hung out with Blake and Leo. He was a trash-talker, but I hushed him up too before he could even say a negative word to me.

Actually, he came up to me and said, "Dang, man, you gonna make the team. You ain't gotta show folks up."

Standing chest to chest, I said, "I'm just running the routes, catching the balls. We don't have any problems, do we?"

"If you keep making me look bad, we gonna have tons of problems. Dang," Landon said.

"I'm out here to win."

"You just got out here." Landon stepped in my face.

I wasn't backing down. "So?"

"All right, all right, boys, pull it apart. Back it up," Coach Strong said. "Look, I guess I should introduce you guys to Amir Knight. He was just tryna get his feet acclimated to the game, but as you guys can see, he has what I already knew: the 'it' factor to be on this field with the Lions. We are a good team, but we can be great if we get another player in the secondary."

"So what, Coach? This chump is just gonna come in and take my job like that?" Colby, a defensive back who had been getting beaten all year, cried out.

Coach Strong nodded. Then he walked back over to the sidelines. Colby held out his hands to the team, wanting people to have his back.

Leo said, "Uh, yeah, I thought I was gonna have to lose some weight and run like a safety the way you been getting killed. We can put the cheerleaders in, and they'd do a better job than you."

"Whatever, man, I was balling. We're winning!" Colby cried out.

I wasn't here to upset anybody. I wasn't here to take anyone's job. I wasn't trying to outshine anybody either. I just wanted to see if I could still do what I did back in middle school. I did want to play, and if Coach would have me, I was willing to put up with the bull to be under the lights on Friday nights.

After practice was over, the quarterback, Blake Strong, said, "Man, I've gotta give it to you, you've got skills. I hope you join the team."

"Why you gotta try to kiss up to him?" Landon asked, walking into the field house beside us.

"Why you gotta be all in my conversation?" Blake said back to his boy.

"I'm just saying, he ain't all that. Dang! He took a couple balls from me. He ain't gonna be doing that on Friday nights against real competition. All of us know we got weak legs from balling twenty-four-seven, and he ain't got nothing." Then Landon turns to me. "What you do? Don't you work at some girls' gym?" he asked.

Guys walking around us looked at me like I had the plague. Leo laughed in the background. I looked over at him, daring him to say something.

"Help me tumble," Leo joked, taking me up on my stare.

Leo went over to Landon, and the two of them tried to do a mock cheer. The rest of the team gathered around and guys laughed hard. I gave a smirk and walked on to the locker room.

Brenton jogged up to me and said, "You straight with all that, right? It's just trash talking. That's what we do."

"Man, I already told you, I got tough skin."

"Amir Knight, come into my office," Coach Strong said.

"Yes, Coach?"

"So what you gonna do? What do you think? This is my team and I want you a part of it. You're not gonna to be popular," Coach Strong said, alluding to the coarse joking.

"I have a brother at home, sir. I'm not here to make friends, Coach," I replied.

"Well, that's what I wanted to let you know. I don't have room on my team for anyone to be on an island. We are one—no showboaters out here. I'm not asking you to take any of these guys by the hand and make them feel good about this transition, particularly Colby whose job I do want you to take, but you must try to get to know the guys to be on my team. You need to blend in. It'll take time, but you should have the heart to try."

"I'm the new kid. They're on the team, sir," I said, feeling like they needed to be cool to me.

"If you want to play football, there are eleven men from one team on the field at all times, not one. Here are the forms I need for you to have your parents fill out. If you're up for that, I'll see you tomorrow with everything signed. I got nothing else to say."

Coach walked out of the door and once again left me to think. He was good at that, but this time I did not know the answer. I wanted to play football, not play in the sandbox with a bunch of whiners; maybe this was not for me.

In my bedroom with all those papers in my hand, I just stared at them. I had a lot of guts being out there on the field doing my thing, but when it came to standing on my feet, going to my parents, and telling them what I wanted to do and what I needed them to sign, I was a wimp. A part of me felt like this was what I wanted; my brother even thought I should try. So maybe I was just overreacting, over thinking, and over dramatizing the situation.

However, a more rational side of me knew I was right on because my dad was going to have a cow, milk it, and then cut it up for meat.

Basically, I knew he would not be happy with my choice, and he would not have any problem letting me know it. Then I thought, why not talk to my mom and let her know what was in my heart? I was not a sissy, but I was a mama's boy. If I buttered her up, she'd get my dad to come around.

The problem with all of this was not only did my dad think football was a waste of time, but if I joined the team, I would have to quit my job. Practice was every day after school, and sometimes on the weekends, so I would have no time to go to Cheertowne, and my dad refused to support me financially besides putting food in my mouth and allowing me to have a place to stay. He gave me no gas money, no money for upkeep on my car, and now that I knew I wanted to do more with Hallie, I was gonna need some funds to take her out. It was the craziest thing in the world that my dad didn't break me off a little somethin' somethin'. Dr. Knight was a surgeon for goodness' sake. We lived in one of the best neighborhoods in Atlanta. Though my car was new, if I had no gas, I couldn't drive it. So I looked at myself in the mirror, thought long and hard about what I really desired deep inside, and asked myself what was I willing to fight for? What was I willing to do without?

Coming to the conclusion that I could not live without football, I picked up the papers and marched into the kitchen. I stood by my mom and put my hands around her waist. I tickled her a little bit and she smiled.

Purring like a cat, she said, "My Amir ..." Knowing I did this move when I was happy since I was little, she said, "Somebody must be in a good mood, playing with his mom like this. I've been so worried about you, son, because I just want you to be happy."

She kissed my cheek. This was right up my alley. I could not have picked better words to come out of her mouth than the ones she actually spoke. She said it: she wanted me to be happy. So I went there. I turned off the water so she'd be able focus on what I had to say.

I took her hands and said, "Mom, thank you for thinking about me, praying for me, and just being there."

"I know it's hard when you and your father get into it and ..."

"I know, Mom. I don't want you to worry about that stuff. I don't want that to be on you. It's for me and Dad. I'm gonna be okay. You raised a tough son."

"I know, baby, but you should not stress. You guys should get along more. I just want things to get better between the two of you guys. I want to help build that bridge. Sometimes I don't know why it's so broken because I know he loves you."

That comment made me look away because I'd often wondered if he did love me. What did I do that was so wrong to make my dad be so horrible to me? I definitely didn't look as much like him as Anthony did, but so what? I looked more like my mom. What was the big deal in that? I did not have the same interests he did, but so what? I was still a decent young man who had good character and morals. I was not one to be in trouble. I was not hanging in the streets or hanging with thugs. Why did he have such a problem with me?

Because I was not on track to make six or seven figures? He hated me because he thought he was going to have to take care of me most of his life. I was sure that was it. What else could it be? My mom's eyes filled with water, and my instinct was to turn off her tears.

I lifted my hands toward her eyes and said, "Mom, please don't cry."

I caught a tear that fell from her eye. She held me tight. Did I have some disease I didn't know about? I could handle my dad. She need not worry.

"Mom, you're saying you want me to be happy. So here, look, I want to play football. I know it's a dangerous sport. I know it's time consuming. However, I know I'm still really good. The coach at my high school is an awesome man who I know Dad will respect. He wants me on his team. I've been out there, I've played—"

"Whoa, whoa, wait, son. Football? Honey, no. That's been over since middle school. You're about to graduate. We need to concentrate on your academics," my mom said, frustrating me.

"Mom, I have a three-point-seven-five; school is not a problem. You just said you wanted me to be happy. Football can do that for me. The only thing I need you to do for me is talk to Dad. It's just a few papers I need you to sign, and maybe if Dad sees that I'm really good at something, better than I was in middle school, he'll relax and let up. He'll let me be a baller. Don't you want to hear your son's name called over the loudspeaker after catching interceptions and running their receivers out of bounds? Just let me play football, Mom. Please talk to Dad."

"Football?!" Both of us were startled when my dad's authoritative voice came into the kitchen and screamed. "Heck no! You're not playing football. That's the stupidest thing I could ever think you would ask to do. You might as well drop out of school right now because football is a game for idiots," my dad said, belittling me.

Trying to keep my cool, I went over to him and said, "Look, Dad, I know you think it's crazy, but I'm really talented at it. I'm sorry I don't want to be a scientist, a engineer, or a doctor, but—"

Cutting me off, he said harshly, "Look, let me just stop you right now. I'm not supporting you to play football. I think it's for idiots. Getting out there and basically hitting each other around, trying to knock each other out for a ball. I'm not agreeing to it. You're not playing, and that's final. Do you understand, Amir?"

my dad said when he came up to my face. "Or do I need to beat the football out of you like I did when you were in the seventh grade?"

Not wanting to give him any respect, I stepped up to him and looked down on him. He might have been smarter than me, but he was not bigger. With every ounce of composure I could muster, I stayed collected. I looked him in the eye and said, "Yes, *man*."

CHAPTER 4

Bad News

The text from Landon King read, "If you think you can hang, come to Wax's party." I was surprised to be invited and that he had my number.

Usually I didn't hang at house parties, but I decided to go. I was so upset with my father, and I knew he would blow a gasket if he knew what I was doing. I felt rebellious, and I was excited to put the address into my GPS and head that way.

My new Ford Mustang was fully loaded. I was pretty particular about where I went because I did not want anyone denting my car or trying to steal it. However, at that moment I felt that because my father bought it, if someone took every single part, I would not care.

Another reason I had no problems show-ing up at the house jam was because I thought Hallie might be there. I really loved the fact that we were having close moments, and she was not pressing me to call her. Since we had space be-tween us, I wanted things to be tighter.

It took me no time to get to the other side of town. There were so many kids in front of Wax's house I did not need my GPS to confirm that I was at the right spot. I parked my ride, made sure it was locked up, saw girls eyeing me like they wanted a ride, and brothers jocking me like they were jealous that it wasn't their car. It always amazed me how people were so into wanting what others had.

"Look who made it, y'all," Landon said as I entered the crowded porch.

"What's up?" I asked, not sure if this was a good idea after all.

"I see you got my text," he said. We slapped hands.

This was interesting because I knew the dude did not like me. Now he was being cool. Was there a catch? Leo and Landon had beers in their hands. They were hanging out with some other football players I had not met yet. I did not know where Brenton and Blake were. However, I thought it was pretty sad that these players thought they had to get drunk to have fun.

Colby, whose spot Coach said I was taking, came up to me and put his hand in my face. "My job, not taken."

His eyes were going in opposite directions. His body was swaying. Clearly he was out of it. I patted him on the back and walked on.

Landon called out, "Where you going?"

"I'll leave you to baby-sit," I said as I continued to head inside.

I was not about to hang with guys I was not even sure were going to be my teammates. The DJ did have the place rocking, and I did not mind getting my dance groove on. If only I could find Hallie and rub up against her fine legs. When my eyes got covered, my heart skipped a few beats. Unfortunately, I turned around and saw it was Lexus, grinning as if I was about to make her every wish come true. I wanted to puke. She was smart though. She had me cornered. She boxed me in with her arms and started whispering stuff in my ear. I did not want to hear any of it.

"I'm just asking for one more chance, Amir. I've been watching you since the moment you came in here. You were huffing and puffing, and I can make your tough walls come down."

I did not entertain Lexus's words. My attention was diverted when I spotted Hallie. My body just seemed to flow toward her or she came to me. Lexus was still talking so I had no real clue as to who came to whom.

Quickly, I was puzzled. It seemed Hallie was more lit than Colby. Her words were slurring, her clothes were not on properly, and she reeked of alcohol. The bartender was a guy named Pinecone who went to our school. I motioned for him to step to me. When he did, I grabbed his collar and almost jerked him across the bar.

"What the heck, dude? Why have you been serving her all of this? If she passes out or something happens to her, it's on you," I yelled, going into protective mode.

"She asked for it, man. What do you want me to do?" Pinecone whined, wanting me to leave him alone.

I let go of his collar in an abrupt way. "You shouldn't be serving drinks in here at all. You know these people are under age."

"What are you, the alcohol police?" Pinecone joked, turning away from me.

From behind, I shouted to Pinecone. "I'ma be your worst nightmare if something happens to her. I'm telling you right now."

"Why?" Lexus demanded.

I saw Hallie talking to some girls on the cheerleading squad, so I knew she was in good hands. However, I wanted to get over there and make sure she was okay. I did not have time for Lexus to trip.

"I'm gonna kill myself if you don't give us one more chance," Lexus said, truly stunning me.

A part of me wanted to say, *Do whatever you have to do*. At least then I would not have to deal with her insane antics. But I was too much of a gentleman to act like her words did not bother me.

Trying to calm her, I said, "Lexus, I don't want you to do anything to harm yourself."

"I know you don't. I know you still care. I know you want to be my guy. Come on, baby, let's leave this place," Lexus said in an insane voice.

I did not know what to say to her. I did not want to send her over the edge, but really she was already too far gone. She could misinterpret everything that I was saying and use it as more fuel to go crazy.

I took a deep breath, placed my hands on both her shoulders, and said, "Look, straight up, you deserve better than me."

"But you're what I want," Lexus pleaded.

"I'm not what you need."

As if I was a real magnet for girls with issues, Hallie place her arms around me and slurred, "I miss you."

One of the cheerleaders, who I think was a twin, said, "I'm Ella. This is Randal. Could you please get our girl home?"

"Didn't you see he was talking to me?" Lexus whined.

"Lexus, let me just help them," I said in a nice way, hoping Lexus would understand.

"Yeah, our friend's in a crisis right now. Can't he just help us?" the short Randal girl said.

Lexus stormed away, and Hallie fell into my arms. I was so mad at Hallie. I tried to get her to tell me where she lived, but she was not making any sense. I asked her girlfriends to go in her purse and give me her driver's license. When I got to my Mustang, I plugged her address into my GPS. This all just seemed so weird. Hallie was just all put together, so sure of herself, so on top of things ... Why was she drunk? It did not do me any good to ask her because she barely knew her own name. It was clear she was mumbling about her mom and that she was going through some serious issues. Instantly, I felt her pain.

When we got to her house, I helped her out of the car. Her hands were all over me. Normally that would have been a good thing, but when I heard her front door slam shut and saw an angry man heading our way, I realized the scene did not look good.

"Who are you? Take your hands off my daughter. What's this? You get girls all loaded up with alcohol and take advantage, or did you slip a roofie into her drink or something? Oh my gosh, my baby daughter's barely conscious," the man howled. "Get off my property right now!"

I was trying to protect his daughter, and here he was accusing me of trying to harm her. He would not let me get a word in edgewise. Hallie could not defend me. This was a mess. Thankfully, her friends pulled up, talked to her father, and explained what happened. I thought he would deem me a hero, but he still wanted me gone. That hurt.

"Oh no, Coach Strong, I'm not having it. My son is not sitting on the bench and being replaced by some new kid that you pulled off the streets," an irate dad was yelling at Coach Strong when I came to football practice.

"With all due respect, Mr. Allen," Coach Strong said with a more level-headed voice, "I know you want Colby to play, and I appreciate all you've done for my program. The bags you bought for my team, priceless ..."

"Don't you forget," Mr. Allen replied.

"But, sir, that was never a bribe to make sure I played your son, was it? If so, I need to get the booster club to refund you your money. Colby is a sophomore. I thought he was ready, and I gave him an opportunity. He hasn't been performing, but the young man that you're talking about is here and can make an impact on the program now. You and I can watch the both of them, and you can tell me whom you think should play. I'm trying to win a championship. Colby will benefit when the scouts come in here and look at all these older guys. Amir and Colby, y'all get on the line. Let's run the forty."

When I got on the line, I looked over and saw Colby was shaking. He said, "Please, please, Amir, don't let me look bad in front of my dad. I know you're gonna take my job. It's yours. I know you're way better than me. I just don't want to look bad. My dad thinks I have skills that I don't have. He didn't even play football, and he's tryna put all this pressure on me. Like he rewrites scripts for Hollywood, he thinks he can write my future."

"Wait, wait, your father is Johnny Allen, the movie producer who lives in Atlanta?"

"Yeah."

"You guys live down the street from us," I said, tripping that I never really played outside to even notice Colby.

I knew exactly what he was going through. Unwanted pressure from a father was too much to bear. So when Coach Strong blew the whistle, I kicked into high gear but immediately pulled back and let Colby beat me.

"See, see, this is exactly what I'm talking about," Mr. Allen called out in dramatic form, like he was the actor and not the producer. "You talking about pulling my son out so some other guy can start who ain't even faster than my boy? What other drills you want to run, Coach? What else do you want to show me? What? What? What!"

Coach looked over at him like, *Man, you do not even got a clue. This dude let your son win.* But Mr. Allen saw what he wanted to see. Though Colby was not truly happy because he knew he did not really beat me, he was not demoralized either. He made his father proud, and that made his chest stick out a few notches.

Coach came over to me and threw his clipboard on the ground and yelled, "What the heck, son? What's going on?"

"I don't know," I lied. "I just slowed up, Coach. I guess."

Coach Strong wasn't buying my response. "Oh, we about to run this again."

"Nah, Coach, he beat me," I said, wanting the results to be left for now.

Coach grabbed my collar, twisted it, and said, "Look, I don't know what game you're playing, but I need you to perform."

I shook my head. I looked over at Colby's father who had two thumbs up pointing at his son. There was no way I was going to take that moment away from Colby. Football meant a lot to me because I was out here against my father's wishes. However, it did not mean more to me than having integrity and not wanting to kick someone when they were down.

"Sir, you might not know this, but fathers can make or break their sons."

Coach looked at me and called out to Colby. "Allen, come here. Do I need to go over there and explain to your father what happened? Or do you want to race again and do it fair and square? I need men on my team, and this guy right here is talented. If you two are on the same team, he's gonna help you get better. Next year when I lose my seniors, you can be in the backfield with Amir. What's it gonna be?"

"Do you," Colby said to me.

I shrugged my shoulders, not knowing what that phrase meant. Coach needed to leave well enough alone. I did not want to hurt this guy.

Leo was close by and said, "That means go for yours. Take no prisoners. Don't feel sorry for him, run."

"You sure?" I asked Colby.

"I gotta learn to stand up to my dad someday," Colby grumbled.

I definitely felt him on that. Coach went back over to stand by Mr. Allen. He blew the whistle, and it was not even close. We did a couple of other drills, like catching passes, taking balls away from the defenders, and every time I outshined Colby Allen. Coach put his hand on Mr. Allen's shoulder. He brushed it off, dropped his head, and walked off from practice.

Coach blew his whistle and everyone started getting in position to go about their normal routine. I could see that Colby was deflated. I did not know the guy, and I was not trying to baby him, but I was concerned. I walked toward him. I was not alone. Blake Strong, the quarterback, was right beside me.

"You gonna talk to him?" Blake asked.

"Yeah. Were you going over there? You can instead," I said to Blake.

"Why don't we both do it?"

"Cool," I said and continued toward Colby.

With all the players moving, it took us a while to see Colby was not on the field. We could not find him anywhere outside. We went over to the field house, and that is when we both stopped in our tracks. Colby's father was going off.

"You're never going to amount to anything, letting this guy come in here and take your starting job. You have no gumption. You're a wimp," Mr. Allen vented.

Colby said, "I don't want to be out here playing ball, Dad. I'm out here because of you."

"Well, there ain't no point of being out here at all when you don't want to do it. Clearly, you can't do it."

"So I can quit?"

His father did not answer that question, but replied, "You disgust me."

It just felt like his dad had a baseball bat and was beating him over the head with it.

"Dang, he sounded like my dad," I muttered.

"Mine too."

The quarterback and I just shared a moment. When Mr. Allen was gone, Blake said to Colby, "It's gonna be all right, man."

"You don't know nothing," Colby cried. "And why were you in here listening to my conversation? Okay, you happy now? My dad thinks I'm worthless. He doesn't give me respect like your pops gives you. And what are you doing standing here, Amir? You got my starting job. If I had your skills ... shoot."

I stepped up to him and said, "I understand. I don't know what Blake's talking about but I understand."

Blake said, "Y'all ain't walked in my shoes. You see my dad coaching, but he has the highest expectations for me. So I know exactly what you're thinking, Colby, what you're feeling, what you're going through, and yeah, I think the only difference is I *do* want to play ball, not for my father, but for me. If you don't want to play ball, you need to let your dad know."

"I want to play, but I just can't play. So sometimes when I know I'm not doing it right, I don't want to be out here. Maybe it's just that I know I'm not very good, so I don't wanna practice or study the playbook. I don't know ... I know he hates me for it, and I don't like that."

"My dad doesn't want me to play, but I want to play for me. He thinks I'm worthless too because I don't have the desire to pick up a scalpel. We can't live the dreams of our fathers. We must live for ourselves. The good news is you have a dad; the bad news is he doesn't really know how to be there for his son, and I just came in here to tell you ... so what. Don't let that ruin you."

I stuck out my hand, Colby slapped it, and Blake nodded. We were all young men with father drama stories. In the Lions' locker room we all made a silent pact to not let the tough demeanor of our fathers demoralize us. Maybe being a part of the football team was not so bad after all.

I had been invited to go with Blake, Brenton, Landon, and Leo to grab a bite to eat. When Blake was with Landon and Leo, he was a little wilder. Brenton and I spent most of our time shaking our heads. Landon tried too hard to be cool. Leo was too cool and hard, and Blake was somewhere in the middle.

"I gotta get home, you guys."

"Wait, no rush, man," Blake said.

"I got to, Blake," I said.

"We just wanted to tell you we're glad you're on the team."

It felt good having them all nod and approve of me, but when I got up and headed to the door, Brenton followed. "Amir, I know you gotta go, but I just wanted to make sure we were cool."

"Just some stuff going on. I'm straight."

"Call me if you need to talk. You got my digits, right?" Brenton asked as I nodded.

When I got to my house, I felt like something was stuck in my throat when I saw my dad's car there. There was another car in the driveway, so I thought hopefully he was entertaining a colleague. I could go my way, and he could stay away.

However, as soon as I walked in the door my dad yelled out, "Amir, is that you? Get in here to this family room right now."

My eyes were wide when I saw Coach Strong standing there. At that moment I knew what all of this was about. When I gave Coach Strong the papers from my parents, I was hesitant. Heck, I was not a liar, but I forged my parents' names. I just thought that even though Coach looked at me weird like, *Are you sure this is on the up and up?* I looked back and sort of made him feel confident; at least I thought I made him feel like everything was legit. Yet here he was, standing in my house bringing the stuff to my parents. What was this about? Coach should have just had my back and left well enough alone.

"Yeah?" I said with a little attitude.

"You see, the Lockwood Lions head football coach is here for a visit. He's been telling your mom and me some very interesting information about you being on his football team and turning in these papers with our signatures of approval on them. The thing is though, son, I haven't signed anything," he said sarcastically. I said nothing as he waited for an explanation.

"So I wonder how my signature got on this paper when I specifically told you that you are not playing on anyone's football team."

Coach held his hands up and said, "Sir, that's why I came by. Dr. Knight, I do respect you and your wife. I just had to make sure it was okay for your son to play on my team."

At that moment I looked at him like, *Man, whatever. You are the one who said you wanted me.* It is not like coaches don't look the other way all the time. They give kids money. They have grades changed. They sweep all kinds of trouble under the rugs. They take care of their players' needs so they can have them on the field. This was nothing new. This was nothing different, and this was nothing that he had to verify.

Coach Strong sensed and saw my anger rising and said, "Amir, don't look at me like that. I can lose my job if I have a player on my team whose parents don't want him to play. However, sir, let me say your son is an incredible athlete."

My dad said, "And, Coach, if you noticed his grades, he's a heck of a student."

I could not believe my father was saying that. He was so hard on me, yet he was defending my academics to the coach. It was certainly a surprise.

"Yes, he's a scholar, and if you couple his academics with his athletic ability, you have something. We still got lots of games to play. Amir has got D1 potential, and the recruiters will be at our school checking out our players because I've got quite a few ballers in his junior class with exceptional potential."

"Well, my son doesn't need an athletic scholarship. He's going to get an academic one. While this D1 might be important to you, it means nothing in this household. If he likes athletics so much, he can be an orthopedic surgeon one day and help them out when they're hurt."

"Is that what your son wants?" Coach Strong asked my father.

My dad stood stern and said, "I hear you have a son, Coach. Do you care what he wants in your home? I imagine you run a pretty tight ship, which is how I run my home. I imagine you handle your team with purpose, which is exactly how I run my operating room. You want the best players, and I look for the best interns coming out of medical school each year. My son is on a different path than football."

When my dad tore up the papers, Coach Strong said, "Sorry I wasted your time. Amir, Mrs. Knight, see you all later."

My father walked him to the door. They shook hands, and my dad shut the door. He gave me a look and briskly came over.

He ranted, "I cannot believe you forged my name, Amir. How could you disregard my wishes? You thought you were going to play anyway. I've always told you things will catch up to you. You can't do things and expect me not to find out. I thought you had so much integrity and that you were a good boy, but you actually forged my name?" he said, pushing me back with his three middle fingers.

Each time he pushed me harder and harder. I was going backwards until I almost fell on the couch. He threw up his hand to slap me, and I was not going to flinch. I wanted him to hit me. I wanted it to be on. It was time for me to show him I was sick of him pushing me around, but he did not slap me. He did not move.

"I can't believe you did that. I can't believe you just signed my name."

So I pushed him back real hard. "Yes, I signed your name. I wanted to play football. I'm almost seventeen. I didn't think I needed your permission. So what? I'm not like you. I don't act like you, and I don't want the same things for myself that you want for me. I'm my own person, Dad."

"Quit calling me that! Quit saying *Dad*, like you're my boy, like you're my son. The reason you don't look like me, the reason you don't act like me … is because you're not my son at all. And stop pushing on me like I'm some kid out there on the football field."

At that moment I do not even know if he knew what he just said. My mom and I were both frozen. Or was she my mom? This whole thing was confusing. He just said that he was not my dad; I was not his son."

"What did you just say?" I asked.

"There's no need for me to sugarcoat it. There's no need for me to act like everything's fine. Sixteen years of pure hell. Tell him, Anna. He's not mine."

I looked at my mom and the tears in her eyes spoke volumes. She did not have to tell me anything. I knew at that moment what he said was true. It all made sense. He never wanted me because I was never his. I was numb and did not know if this was good news or bad news.

CHAPTER 5

Unexpected Ending

So you're not my father?" I asked, waiting on an answer from the man who raised me for sixteen years.

He looked over at my mom. She was a basket case. Her face looked like the world had turned upside down. Immediately, my dad wanted to make it right. He came over to me and changed his tune all together.

My dad pleaded, "I'm so sorry. Please, forgive me. That's not what I meant."

As he stepped closer to me, I backed away. I asked him a question, but suddenly I did not want to know the answer. However, I certainly did not want him to try and cover it up. No apologies needed.

"How could you do this, Anthony? How could you ruin us like this?" my mom called out.

He tried to go over and console her, but she was beyond wanting empathy. It was the first time I saw how much he cared for her. He truly did not want to let her down. However, emotions were too high. Frustration reared its ugly head.

"Fine, fine, fine," he screamed and stormed off, leaving the two of us in the family room.

My mother plopped down on the couch. Her face showed how devastated she was. However, I needed the whole truth.

I took her hand, kneeled down, and said, "Mom, what is he talking about? Did you adopt me?"

"No, baby," she quickly responded.

"You are my biological son." She kissed my face a few times.

I squeezed her hand to encourage her to continue.

I said, "Mom, come on, talk to me. Is Anthony Jr. Dad's kid? He looks just like Dad."

She wiped her eyes and said, "Sit beside me, baby. You're almost seventeen. I've wanted to talk to you about this for a while. Your dad didn't want me to …"

Angrily I screeched, "Don't call him my dad if he's not my dad."

"He *is* your father. Though he gets angry and upset, he wanted you to know the truth, but he kept saying things were fine and to leave them alone. He was treating you so ugly though."

"Mom, can you just explain to me what's happening? What's going on?"

She took a deep breath and said, "Anthony is your dad's child and my child. We were married and at first things were great. But early on in his residency, he was keeping long hours at the hospital. I found out that he had affairs with a few nurses. Back then we lived in an apartment building that had a lot of young families. We organized a play group, and there was one stay-at-home dad who kept saying nice things to me. To get back at your father, I was with him one time."

The news she was giving me was heavy. I was the product of an affair. I didn't really know how that made me feel.

"Your dad and I had not been together, so he knew immediately when I came up pregnant that it was not his child. He took responsibility because a lot of it was his fault."

"So he made you go sleep with someone who wasn't your husband?" I said sarcastically to my mom. She took her hand and smacked me.

"Forget it." I got up and went to my room. She immediately followed me.

"Amir, I'm sorry. I deserved that. I didn't mean to slap you. It was terrible, but I was not going to have an abortion. It was my mistake, but I loved my baby," my mom said. She stroked my face gently and continued, "I loved you from the moment I found out you were growing inside me. I wasn't going to prevent you from coming into this world. I told your father I would get a divorce, but he didn't want that. I don't know … I think he hoped the baby would be a girl, and she'd look just like me. But you were you and did not look like me. He hired a private investigator and found out whom I'd had the affair with. He had pictures of the man, and as you got older, you grew from looking cute and innocent to looking more like this man. It just made your father explode."

"Well, he doesn't have to worry about it anymore," I said. I grabbed a duffle bag from my closet.

"What are you doing?" my mom asked in a panicked voice. "You're not leaving this house, Amir. You are not going anywhere. I love you. You're my son, and—"

"And what, Mom? And what?"

My dad came to the door and said, "And you shouldn't have to leave, son. I'm going to go. I overstepped my boundaries, and I'm leaving for a while."

With a suitcase in his hand, he went to the door as my mom followed him. I fell to my knees and let out tears I was unable to hold back. My mom came back in my room after I heard the front door close. She was on the telephone.

She rubbed my back, and I raised my head when I heard her say, "Hi, Coach Strong, this is Mrs. Knight. You were over not too long ago, and we were discussing Amir. I've decided to let him play. If you will still have him on your team, he'll be at practice tomorrow." There was a pause. "Yes, he's right here. Coach wants to speak to you," my mom said, handing me the phone.

My eyes went from crying to smiling, "Hello, Coach?"

Enthusiastically, Coach Strong said, "Amir, this is great news, young man. I hope there are no hard feelings. I definitely had to make sure that it was cool for you to be on my field. The Lions need you. I need to have an understanding that you won't lie to me again, son. This coach-player relationship only works when there is honesty. Is that okay with you? Are you ready to play for Lockwood? Are you ready to win a state title?"

"Yes, sir, I'm ready," I answered with excitement in my voice.

He questioned, "You sure?"

"Sir, I've been holding back my urge to get on the football field for a very long time. You saw that I have potential, and you believed in me. I'm gonna give you all I've got. I assure you I'm ready."

"Well, that sounds great. If your mom can bring you to practice to sign the papers, then that's great."

"Yes, sir, Coach."

"Tell your father I said thanks. He'll see that football is not so bad."

I held the phone for a minute and said, "Okay, Coach."

"Everything okay?"

"Not really. But I'd rather not talk about it," I said, knowing he asked me to be honest.

"Then let's leave it all for the field. You put your aggression there, and it'll be okay."

"Thanks, Coach."

"Keep your head up. I'll see you tomorrow."

When we hung up the phone, I looked at my mom and said, "Mom, you didn't have to do that."

"Yes, I did. It's about time I stood up for my son and allowed him to do some of the things that are in his heart. There are many things in this life that you can be great at. You can be a great lawyer. You can be a great teacher. You can be a great doctor, and you can be a great athlete. Not everyone has the skills, but if you have the talent, then I'm behind you. I should've stood up for you a long time ago," she said with some shame.

Lifting her chin, I said, "Sorry about all this, Mom."

She hugged me tight, like she wasn't sure that she'd ever see me again. "Don't you leave me," she said, confirming how I knew she felt.

"I don't want you to go anywhere until it's time for you to go off to college. Are we clear?"

I looked her in the eyes. I could not believe she stuck up for me, going out on a limb to give me my dream. She even allowed my dad to walk out to restore some peace. Regardless of all the things I had to work out with my dad, I knew without a doubt that I had a mom who loved me and supported me one hundred percent.

"Mr. Wan, thank you for taking my call," I said to my boss at Cheertowne before school started.

"You say important, Amir. I listen. No problem to make sure you okay," he said with his Asian accent.

"Sir, I've had a remarkable opportunity to have a job at your gym. Helping kids fly has been rewarding. I know putting up with me has been a lot."

"Yeah, you not on time always. You play in my gym always. I sometimes don't know who's teacher and who's student, but you good, Amir. Please, don't tell me you go."

"Mr. Wan, I think I'm gonna try my hand in sports at school. I'm an eleventh-grader, and the football coach wants to use me on his team. I know I'm scheduled for this week. I don't ever cut out on my responsibilities, and since it's the last minute, I will be there."

"No, I play pigskin long ago too when I first got here. I love game. Will come see you play if not benchwarmer," Mr. Wan teased.

I laughed and said, "I should be playing, sir."

"Just remember, Amir, nothing given to you in this life. I have high expectations. Make sure you work hard because I want you always remember you can't just cruise control life. You work hard. Now go be ready for some football."

My first class was gym. I could not help but to search around for Hallie. Her class with Coach Woods was going outside to run around the track. My class with Coach Strong was staying in to do gymnastics. I was in my element. I could do the rings. I could vault. I could certainly tumble on the floor. I do not know why, but I just did everything I could to the max. Certainly, I was not trying to show off because I knew showcasing my skills would label me a jerk. I would have guys calling me queer and stuff. However, after I finished tumbling, Brenton and a few guys from the football team rushed up to me with just the opposite reaction.

"All right!"

"Sweet!"

"We want learn."

I was shocked. Maybe that was a lesson to me. Don't have expectations or do not think things are gonna be one way or the other, just go out, stay in your lane, and execute. When you give it all you got and leave it all out on the floor, you can get high marks in life.

I went over to the drinking fountain to catch my breath and get some water. Coach Strong came up to me and said, "Amir, thanks for showing these guys that gymnastics is cool."

I spotted Lexus. She appeared all broken up at that point. I was barely listening to Coach Strong because I was so distracted.

"Are you okay, son? If you ever want to talk about anything, my door is open. I can't have my players putting their minds elsewhere. Waxton, don't grab the rings like that, boy. You'll hurt yourself," Coach said before having to go back over to the class.

He did not even see Lexus. She was in the corner behind some bleachers, sobbing. Taking a deep breath, I stepped over to her, knowing I should stay away.

She said, "I don't want to be here anymore."

"If you don't feel good, go to the nurse. You can check out of school, I'm sure," I responded. What was she getting at?

"I don't wanna be home. I don't wanna be at the gym. I don't wanna be at school. I don't wanna be anywhere. If I can't have you, I want to die. See, look," she said. She turned the insides of her palms toward me, and I saw blood gushing from both her wrists."

"Oh my gosh, Lexus. What did you do, girl?" I said in amazement at the disturbing view.

A pocket knife dropped from her fingers. It was clear that she was serious. This was too much.

"Watching you out there looking so fine in those shorts and not giving me a chance, I just don't want to be here. Can you hold me one last time?" Lexus uttered.

There was no way I could ever have predicted Lexus would try to end her own life. I mean, I was just a guy. There was nothing special about me. If I didn't want to be with her, she should have enough pride to want to be around for herself. She could always find another guy. If her life was over, she would devastate so many people in the process. Immediately I took off my shirt, ripped it in two, and covered up her wrists. I had taken CPR as a prerequisite to work at Cheertowne. Though we never studied self-inflicted knife wounds, I did know that the bleeding had to be stopped.

"You care," she squealed. "You care."

I got her from under the bleachers and yelled, "Coach Strong, help! Anybody, help!"

Brenton heard me first and rushed over in my direction. "What's up, man?"

"Get your uncle! Get a phone! Dial nine-one-one!" I yelled. I saw the color draining from Lexus's face. Man, I was not worth it.

Mayhem broke out. Coach rushed over. A group of us shielded her from prying eyes. Though Lexus was weak and barely conscious, she knew she was holding on to me. Every time Coach tried to take over and allow me to step away, she squealed as if it physically pained her to be away from me. It was super creepy.

I just wanted to take her and shake her. I got that life was hard. Though I did not know her life, and I did not know what she was going through, she kept hollering that I did not want her anymore. Surely that was *not* enough for her to want to leave this world. To me that rationale was ridiculous.

When she closed her eyes, Coach got me to step back. Coach Woods came rushing in, and she started taking care of Lexus. When the paramedics took her, Coach called me to his office.

"You, come here, we need to talk. Right now!" he insisted. "Shut the door. Tell me what happened with you and this girl."

Being clear, I said, "I didn't cut her wrists if that's what you're asking."

"I know that. But when I was talking to you earlier, you were preoccupied and looking over to where the girl was found. Talk to me," he said.

"Yeah, 'cause I saw her crying. Obviously she hurt herself really bad. When I went over to her, she turned her arms to me, and all I saw was a bunch of blood. It freaked me out, Coach," I tried to explain. He looked at me like he wanted the other part of the story about how I was connected to her. "I admit it; I dated the girl. She wouldn't take no for an answer, and she's been stalking me. I believe she slashed my tires, and she showed up at my house uninvited at two thirty in the morning. It's been overwhelming. I told her in no uncertain terms that I didn't want to talk to her anymore. Then she goes and does this. She said she didn't wanna live. All of this is my fault." I put my hand on my head and dropped into the chair.

Trying to calm me, Coach said, "One thing I learned as an educator of high school students is that you see some unpredictable stuff. You can't blame yourself for someone else's actions. Obviously the girl is dealing with some issues and needs some serious help. I'm glad you wrapped her arms though. You stopped the bleeding as much as you could."

"I just hope she's all right. If she dies—"

Coach Strong cut me off and said, "Don't even go there. Don't even think about it. Okay?"

"Yes, sir." I nodded.

"Okay," he responded shakily.

I was truly surprised when Hallie's dad called and invited me to dinner. Now here I was, driving over to their house. Last time I saw him, he was ordering me off his property. Though that was a few days ago, for him to be so nice and extend this type of invitation just blew me away.

It actually worked well because I did not want to be home. Even though my dad—or the person who raised me, or the guy who didn't like that I was somebody else's son, or whatever I was supposed to call him—was not home, it was still awkward. Also, I wanted to take my mind off of the Lexus scare. Word was she was physically fine, but it was still a big ordeal that I didn't want to think about.

I was walking to the door, and I was just a little nervous. A car pulled up in the driveway after me. It appeared that I was not the only guest for the evening. A nice-looking lady about my mom's age got out of the car. She seemed as nervous as I was, fixing her dress and hair as she walked up.

"I figured I'd wait on you. We're going to the same place and no need in making them answer the door twice," I said, making small talk.

"No, you were just a little too nervous to go in by yourself," she joked. "I'm Greta."

"I'm Amir," I said, shaking her hand.

"Here we go. You make sure your girlfriend takes it easy on me, and I'll make sure my boyfriend doesn't come down too hard on you dating his daughter," she said. She gave me a quick tap on the back.

Both Hallie and Mr. Ray greeted us. Mr. Ray nodded. Hallie took my hand and led me to the couch.

When we were alone, she said, "I'm so glad you're here. I can't believe my dad is making me have dinner with this lady."

I wanted to say she seemed nice, but I knew women a little better than that. I liked Hallie, but I was not trying to cosign on all of her thoughts. However, I also did not want her to think I was against her either.

"Hallie, don't keep him over there all to yourself. Let the boy breath a little bit," her father teased.

"I'm so sorry I was wasted the other night," she whispered in my ear before we walked toward her father and Greta.

I whispered back, "It's cool. You said that over the phone when we talked. We're straight."

"So, Amir ... your last name?" her dad asked.

"It's Knight, sir."

Mr. Ray said, "Amir Knight, hmm okay, and your parents? What do they do? You have any siblings? Tell me a little bit about yourself."

"You don't have to grill the young man," Greta said to him.

"I just want to get to know him. I won't be too hard on him. I think we have already been down that road a few days ago."

"When you overreacted," Hallie said, showing me she had my back.

Her dad grunted, "Don't get started."

"What happened a couple of days ago?" Greta asked.

Hallie yelled out, "None of your—"

I grabbed her arm.

"Ouch."

"You gotta be nice to the lady," I said, knowing Greta and I had a pact.

I certainly did not want to talk about my parents. I knew Greta did not want to have her boyfriend's hostile daughter on her hands. Hallie needed to chill.

"Tim, let's let these two talk. I can go in the kitchen and help you finish dinner. We can eat in a second. We can all get to know each other then."

Hallie turned on some music so her father couldn't hear what we were saying. She sat down close to me and took my hand.

"I know you might have been outside, talking to the lady all of thirty seconds, but please don't try to stop me from being me again. I don't like her, and I'm not going to be civil."

"Your dad likes her. Doesn't that count for something?" I said, realizing I couldn't be the just-get-along, go-along companion.

In a weird way, Hallie already gave me a reason to try athletics again. I did not want any woman totally controlling me. I had my man card, and I did not want anyone taking it from me. I was not ever going to be disrespectful toward her, but if I did not agree with her, she needed to be cool with that.

"I thought you were supposed to be on my side," she said, getting a little testy.

"And who says I'm not?" I whispered into her ear.

I liked her spunk though. It attracted me. I leaned in for a quick kiss, and she settled down. Laughter came from the kitchen, and the last thing I wanted to have happen was for her father to walk in and see more going on than there was. We'd been there and he'd assumed that.

"You don't have to worry about me not being in your corner," I told her. "Just because we don't always agree doesn't mean that I'm not in your corner. I'm just giving you another perspective."

"It's easy for you to say, parents giving you the benefit of the doubt, whatever. Your home life is great; mine is a mess. It's just been me and my dad for the longest, and I can't think about it changing."

I looked away. I walked over and looked at some of the pictures on the fireplace mantle. I wanted to talk to Hallie and tell her all that was going on with me. However, there was so much going on that I did not even know how to put it into words. I was now playing football and while I knew she would think that was great, I did not know if I would cut it during game time. I did not want her to know until I was sure I would be sticking it out. Also, I could not tell her that the parents she thought were perfect were not my parents in totality. Nor did I want her to know the jealous other trainer at Cheertowne just tried to take her own life because I broke it off. Clearly she had her own drama. As the guy in the relationship, I did not want to make it worse.

"I'll be right back," she said, excusing herself.

Her father walked in from the kitchen and said, "Can I talk to you for a sec?"

"Yes, sir," I said, clearing my throat.

"I really wanted to thank you for being an upstanding gentleman. It must not have been easy for you having me jump down your throat like I did. All you tried to do was help my child. You could've taken advantage of her, but you didn't. You saw to it that she got home safely. I just want to let you know that I'm forever grateful. I'm really appreciative and thankful that she's got you in her life. She likes you and I just don't ..."

Helping him not have to go on, I said, "I got you, sir. I have no intention of hurting your daughter."

"I must meet your parents," Mr. Ray said. "They've raised you right."

Fifteen minutes later, we were all eating our dinner. Quickly life got a little out of hand when the doorbell started ringing nonstop. Mr. Ray was irate when he answered the door and saw a homeless-looking lady standing there demanding to come in. I did not have to guess it was Hallie's mom. She rushed over to her, but her father stepped in between the two of them.

Greta and I looked back at each other; we could not believe what we were witnessing. There was a mother who badly wanted to hold her child, but there was also a protective father who did not want someone stoned to hurt his baby. They both seemed genuine, but who was right? Who was wrong?

Once again Hallie's dad flipped a switch and became the upset man I had met a few days before when he kicked me off of his property. This time he threw Hallie's mom out of the house, and she was kicking and screaming.

"Why won't you let me see my mom? Why won't you let me talk to my mom? I can't believe this," Hallie screeched.

"She comes to my house higher than an airplane. She doesn't get to come here any time she wants, and she certainly is not allowed to come here like this."

Her dad put himself up against the door. Hallie tried to push him out of her way. She was screaming. He was yelling. I could hear her mom on the other side of the door kicking it and wanting to come in. I wanted to help, but this was not my business.

We were eating a peaceful meal that was abruptly interrupted. At that point no one was hungry. Dinner was over with an unexpected ending.

CHAPTER 6

Start Connecting

I knew I really cared for Hallie Ray because seeing her cry uncontrollably really affected me. If I could have taken all of her pain away, I would have. However, I had no say in what was going on. I desperately wanted to come to her rescue, even as she argued back and forth with her father to allow her to help her mom. He would not grant her request.

Deeply wanting to intervene, I mustered up the strength to say, "Sir, I can help."

Hallie quit hitting her dad. She immediately turned in my direction. She looked over at me.

"Thank you," Greta said to me. "Seeing the two of them go at it like this is too much to bear."

Mr. Ray stood there waiting for me to speak, so I said, "Sir, I have my car, and I can take Hallie around to look for her mom. She couldn't have gotten too far. I can be with her to make sure nothing happens, and I'll bring her right home."

"No, no, she doesn't need to find her mom. They don't need to talk. Thank you, but this is none of your business."

"Come on," Greta said. She went over to Mr. Ray and tried making him see logic.

"Dad, you don't want me to go by myself," Hallie rationalized. "Amir is very responsible. He brought me home when I was drunk, for goodness' sake. Please, let him go with me, Dad. You can see he's got muscles. Nobody's gonna bother me. He'll bring me right back."

"I don't want you to see he has muscles," Mr. Ray said to his daughter. "And you saw what kind of state your mom was in. Besides, if you find her, what are you going to do?"

"I don't know, Dad," Hallie said, as the tears continued to fall.

"I just want to tell her that I love her and that she can get out of this crazy life. She doesn't have to let drugs control her. Please, just give me a chance to try. That's all I'm asking. She came here for a reason."

Mr. Ray vented, "Yeah, to get money so she can use it to get even more stoned. She probably hated that we were here. She probably wanted to break in and steal like she's done before. Your mother's a loser and ..."

At that point I could not even hear what Mr. Ray was saying. To hear someone call someone else a loser, even when they deserved it, was hard to take. I could not defend Hallie's mom either. What idiot would leave their family for drugs? However, I did not walk in her shoes, so I could not cast any judgment. I could see from Hallie's point of view that her mother did not deserve such a harsh label from her father. So regardless of what her dad thought, I came behind his angel and put my arms around her.

I looked at her father and said, "I got her, sir. We'll be right back."

It was not like I needed his permission at that point. There would have been a terrible scene if he would have stood in our way, but Hallie was not going to stop until she found her mom. We were not kids. We had our own minds, and our parents needed to deal with that. Seeing we were serious, he stepped out of the way. Greta opened the door.

As soon as we got outside, Hallie jumped on me. That was a complete turnaround. She'd gone from mad to glad. She kissed me all over my face. I could see her dad was looking out of the window, so I pulled away.

"Let's go find your mom." I grabbed her hand, and we got to my car before her father could change his mind.

"You just don't know what this means to me," she said, hugging my neck. "For you to stand up to my dad like that, and for you to basically let him know regardless of what he thought, we were going. Oh my gosh, Amir ... you're awesome. Who cares that you don't play football? You're tougher than any guy I know. My dad included. That's why he opened up the door. He knew he couldn't stop us. Thank you."

The last thing I wanted to be was disrespectful to anyone's father. Particularly the father of the girl I really liked. I was not second-guessing my decision, but I did not like that Hallie was making such a big deal out of it. I was not trying to defy her dad. I just wanted him to care about what his daughter was going through. I needed him to know that it bothered me that she was breaking. I wanted him to see that I was going to be there when things got rocky for his child, but I was not sure if that was how he saw it at all.

As we drove around for an hour searching for her mom, I knew my task was going to be harder than I had imagined. Hallie was already a basket case. None of my efforts were helping to put her together. Her father had a point. Could we handle it if we found her mom? Sure, Hallie thought I was tough, but if we ran into some drug dealers equipped with guns, I did not stand a chance.

I nearly passed out when I searched the crack house where Hallie's mom was known to frequent. I could not believe my girl had entered such an awful place. It was filthy and danger-ous. I vowed that Hallie would never ever search these streets by herself again.

After we were done searching without suc-cess, I pulled into a nearby park. I had to get Hallie to settle down. She was rightfully upset about her mom. But she was scaring me. I did not want her to cry so hard. I stroked her hair. I rubbed her back. I wiped her cheeks. I put my face next to hers, and then we started kissing. Then the kisses got deeper. She was beginning to take off her shirt, and I realized that she was all intense with the physical interaction that she was once again misplacing all that she was feeling.

"Stop," I said, pulling back to my side of the car. "Let's not do this."

"What? Why are you stopping me? Why are you pulling back? I know what I want. I want to be with you. I want to forget all about this."

"Exactly, you want to forget all about this. You don't really want to be with me."

"Yes, I do. You stood up to my dad. You cared for me when I was drunk."

"Exactly! Why did you get drunk? Because you were all upset about your mom. You have got to deal with that. You can't turn to alcohol or sex and think everything's going to be okay. It's just not that easy."

"Why? Because I woke up with a massive headache after that night? Or is it because if I have sex with you now, I'm going to regret it tomorrow? Is that what you think? I'm not going to regret being with you. This is different. I really care about you, Amir. Please, touch me, feel me, and make me feel good."

"No," I told her sternly and truly meant it. "I've got stuff going on with me right now too."

"Well, it's not heavier than what I'm dealing with," she said, having no clue.

Now was not the time for me to go into it with her because clearly she was only all into herself. Her world was a little upside down. I was not trying to pin my issues with hers, but I was also not thinking that a physical interaction would make both of us feel good when we both had such deep issues. I'd slept with one girl to satisfy my urges, and I'd never do that again.

"You don't want to be with me? Fine, don't call me anymore! Take me home now, and never freaking speak to me again," she pouted.

I did not know if that was a scare tactic. I did not know if she thought that was going to make me change my mind. I did not know what she was thinking, but I could only take her at face value. So I drove her home in silence. When we pulled up in her driveway, she did not say bye and neither did I. She got out, slammed the car door shut, walked away, and never looked back. We had been connecting so well, and now there was nothing between us. Still, I knew I did the right thing, even if I lost her.

"Quit trying to showboat!" Waxton yelled out to me. I was doing what I'd always done in practice: take balls away.

"Please, you better get out of my face. Just because you are not on your game, don't hate because I'm on mine."

When we ran the next play, Waxton and an offensive lineman did not cover their assignments and purposely ran full speed into me. Imagine getting hit by a three-hundred-pound offensive tackle and a two-hundred-ten-pound running back who benched three hundred fifty pounds. I was taken out pretty hard. There were a lot of oohs and aahs going on around me. I did not know if I was out for a second or a few minutes, but as soon as I came to, I immediately tried to get up. But I was a little too groggy to do so.

Brenton stood over me and said, "Hey, take it easy."

I flung his hand off of me and said, "Stop, I don't need your help. I don't need your hand. I can get up on my own. Waxton, if you want to take it all the way there, bring it, guy. Let's just go for it." I looked around for the running back who thought he was all that.

The guy could play, but his grades sucked. His attitude was even worse. Whoever told him he was the man inflated his head a little too much. The balloon was about to pop, and I had the needle. He was just a jerk. His coarse joking was over the top. If you did not laugh at what he said, he made it a point to come after you. He was a real insecure dude. As the pieces of the puzzle started to unfold, I realized a few of the defensive linemen were in on the brutal tactics. They were giving each other high-fives and were over with Wax, whispering.

I immediately ran over there and said, "What? Y'all didn't want to block your man? Y'all wanted him to hit me? I'm not here for you to like me. I don't need you to block for me. I don't even need you to play fair—"

"I, I, I, I!" Coach Strong yelled. "There is no *I* in team, Amir. How about you head over to my office right now. The rest of you guys get back to work, now!"

"Why I got to go to your office, Coach? They ganged up on me. My body was the one just on the ground. Their behinds were the ones not performing out there, and I got to come to your office," I grumbled.

"Look, I don't need any lip from you. Now zip it up and take it to my office, now."

Storming off, I went into his office. He told me to have a seat on the couch. He was not happy either, but at that point, I did not care. I had not pushed anybody back. I had not given them what they gave to me. I did not deserve to be having a talk.

"Amir, I told you, I don't have any show-boaters on my team," Coach lectured.

"Coach, I was just playing ball. I didn't get in anybody's face and harass them for missing their assignment. Nah, that's Waxton. I just capitalized on it. Boom! I took the ball. I am the man! I'm not the showboater."

"No, I have the right one in here. You kept saying I, I, I. When we go out there Friday night and I ease you into the game because I know

I'm going to need you, I want you to be ready to cover your assignments. While you got a good knack for the ball, sometimes you don't stay in your lane, and you could be faked out."

"But when has that happened, Coach?"

"This is just practice. You haven't faced a defender yet. What happens if your instinct is wrong, and you think he's throwing the ball one way but the ball is coming to the lane you abandon? The receiver will be open, catch the ball, and we'll get burned. That might not be a big deal if we got a forty-something point lead, but the teams we're about to play the next stretch of the season, they're animals on offense and beasts on defense. So I doubt that we'll be running up the score on anybody, nor do I want the other team to run it up. I need you to *do you* and stop hating on these guys because they've got camaraderie."

"I don't hate that."

"You act like you do. Something inside of you doesn't want to get along with anybody here. Can you be a team player, Amir? You need to talk to me. You need to tell me what's going on right here and right now. You are bringing a lot of pent-up frustration to my team and my practices, and you might not have been able to see that there was something practically stuck up your butt, but I'm the one to pull it out. We got a game to win. Talk to me."

Why in the world would I want to talk to him? All he was doing was screaming like my dad. I had spent enough time with Blake for him to tell me that his dad was not winning the best father in the world award. Also, dealing with Coach Strong myself, I knew he wasn't winning the nicest coach of the year award either.

"Is it that your dad doesn't want you to play? Your mom is the one who called me, and all I needed was one parent to sign the forms. I know your dad was pretty strong about his feelings on football. If you are taking crap at home because of this decision, I'll talk to him again."

Coach Strong kept going on, saying your dad, your dad, your dad, your dad. Finally, I just blurted out, "Just found out he's not my dad, okay?"

Coach sank in his chair and was silent. He did not push me to talk. Clearly by his mannerisms, I could see he wanted the full story.

"Amir, I'm a tough coach ..." Coach Strong said after minutes went by and neither of us said a word. "But my former players will tell you—and even the ones here know—I care deeply about my athletes. You got an issue or a problem, then I want to try and fix it. I'm about winning football games, but I know I have been called to this job to make men. You can't run from your problems."

That sounded good, but it was hard to hit something head on when it's been thrown in your face so hard. However, this was eating me up. Maybe he did have a method to his madness.

I opened up. "I learned not too long ago that my mom had an affair. My dad knew. I'm the product of the affair, and they kept me."

I gave him the full details of how it all came out. I was glad that he came from behind his desk, sat on the couch, and really listened to me. It felt good to talk.

"So how do you feel about all of this?"

"I don't know. It's admirable that he ac-knowledged me as his son, but it's horrible that he has treated me like dirt all my life. It shows he has regretted his decision. I guess I would probably feel better if he would have gotten rid of me one way or another. If I wouldn't have existed, it wouldn't have mattered anyway. And if he would've given me up for adoption, at least I would've been with loving people who wanted to take on the responsibility, not with someone trying to be a knight in shining armor, but failing to live up to their last name. Why me?"

"Son, so many players on my team have issues with their dads. You're not alone in that regard."

"What does that have to do with anything, Coach?"

"It means that there are a lot of young men out there hurting like you, and football is such an aggressive sport that you get out there and the emotions that you're dealing with outside of the game come into play. Everybody gets a little too worked up sometimes. We have to keep each other in check."

"I can't be there for them if I can't be there for myself."

"You're right. I'm not going to pretend that I have all the answers. I'm a father who gets it wrong too, but you're a level-headed young man with a lot of potential, a lot of heart, and a lot of guts. The tenacity to forge your dad's signature—"

I quickly cut him off and said, "He's not my dad."

"You know what I'm saying. For you to do that showed you really wanted to be here, and now that you have a legitimate opportunity to play, don't let anything distract you from that. Be open to meeting new people. Be able to allow your dad to deal with whatever he's feeling about the situation. Look for the good in all circumstances. Don't hate, but love. When you do that, you're going to be open to more possibilities for yourself. Right now you're frustrated that the doors are blocked, but you're the one who's standing in your own way. Fix you and you'll fix your problems."

He walked out, leaving me to ponder his thoughts. Darn, he was good. Now, how would I respond?

"Hey, man, um, if you're not up to anything, I could use a partner to go with me, to a Big Brother Big Sister meeting," Brenton stepped into his uncle's office and asked me.

"Huh?" I said, looking up at Brenton, who I guess was trying to be friendly again.

He explained, "Blake and I volunteer down at the YMCA. We're teaching some of the little boys the fundamentals of football. Today he's got to do some extra studying. He's the one with the car. So I figured instead of me just canceling, I'd see if you wanted to swing by there. It's only an hour session, but it makes a difference to the kids."

"You volunteer?" I said, actually impressed with that.

Brenton nodded. I agreed to go. After we stopped at Church's Chicken, we were there.

"I love coming to this club because most of these boys don't have fathers. I can relate to that," Brenton said. "I never knew my dad."

Certainly Coach Strong's office was not bugged so that all the boys in the locker room could overhear what we had talked about, but it was sort of eerie that Brenton immediately started talking about boys with no fathers. That was exactly the situation I was in. Just great, but I did not want to open up, so I looked out of the window.

"Amir, I know that's not your issue, but volunteering and giving back is always good. I know you got a good dad, so just imagine if you didn't."

"How old are they?"

"They range in ages, but the groups we work with, they're eight- and nine-year-olds."

"So I imagine they don't want you to take pity on them, but they may be a little angry and upset they are fatherless. Each of them probably thinks they are going to be the next NFL great."

"You're pretty much dead on for someone who can't relate," Brenton said.

I could have clarified things with Brenton. I could have let him know that I now had no clue who my father was. I could have revealed that I, too, was very angry and did not want anyone to take pity on me. However, I stayed quiet.

We got into the YMCA, and it was time for me to pour into others and change my perspective as Coach Strong advised. I needed to make somebody else smile. I knew if I focused on what was going on with me, I'd be frowning from here to South America.

When we got going, I had four kids who were eight years old. We were going to be playing against the four nine-year-olds Brenton was coaching. It was just flag football, but he and I knew we were both competitive and had been champions in flag football in PE. Just because we switched to coaching, our desire to win was not going to disappear. Brenton was eyeing me like he wanted to win, and I was eyeing him like my team was going to cream his boys even though mine were younger.

We had a blast seeing the boys run around, asking us questions about how to hold the ball, talking to them about why we loved football so much, and then seeing their faces light up when we gave them tickets to our next home game. When we had to wrap the session after a tie, we brought all the boys around. We asked them if there was anything that they wanted to talk about.

There was a little boy named Jake who stood when no one else wanted to and said, "I haven't been able to sleep the last couple of nights. See, my mom and I live in the basement, and my aunt and uncle live on top with their two kids. I have been wondering for the past couple of years why my dad wouldn't be there for me like my uncle is there for my cousins ..."

Brenton's head dropped, and I did not know much of the story about him and Blake, but I was sure that it had to be a struggle for him; having a tough but loving uncle was not like having a father.

"Brenton, you want to take this one?" I said to him

"That's not all," the little boy Jake said, cutting me off.

"Oh, I'm sorry."

"Well, we had to move out last week. When I started asking questions, nobody had answers. We sat around for a family meeting, and I learned the man who I thought was my uncle was really my dad. He was just taking care of us because he didn't want to pay child support. He did not want my mom to take him to court and stuff, but now I know his wife doesn't want me there."

I could not believe what I heard. His situation was worse than mine. This kid was only eight. It just did not seem right. I had to give him hope.

I looked at Jake and said, "Come on, sport. Let's go shoot some hoops."

Jake smiled. Brenton nodded. Jake and I got up and walked away from the others.

"Can I share something with you?" I said to him. "I just learned the man I was living with is not my father, and you just learned that man you're living with is yours. There's a lot of tension in my home too, but I don't want you to think what's going on with the adults is your fault. What happened to bring us into this world doesn't have to control our lives. I know your mother loves you, and while your father hid the truth from you, I know things will get worked out right."

"You think he'll want to be my dad like he is to his other two kids?"

"I hope so, Jake, but I know whether he does or doesn't that you're a pretty cool little dude. You will be fine. Want to play some basketball?"

He nodded. I let him beat me. He was even happier.

When I was taking Brenton home, he said, "So you were able to connect with that guy. You wanna talk about anything?"

"Just my world turned upside down, that's

all. I found out that the good old Dr. Knight isn't my dad."

"Dang, man, I'm sorry."

"No, it actually explains a lot. Coach Strong gave me some really good advice."

"Yeah, my uncle wants to help us grow up right."

"How have you been able to do it, not having a dad?" I asked.

"My uncle has been good. Even with that, I realize he's not my dad. So I try not to compare myself to Blake. It used to be harder when I was younger, but Blake would always get in so much trouble that it was easy for his dad to think I was better. It made Blake madder than it made me. I guess I know I can't change what has happened with my upbringing, but I made a vow to myself to make sure that I'm responsible in that area. I won't make babies too early or with somebody that I don't really want to be with. I'm living every day thinking about the future, and I know that it's harder when kids don't have a dad, or they have a dad who's a deadbeat. It's a much easier life when their dad is there and when he provides. So your dad might not be yours biologically, but from where I sit, he set you up pretty nice. All right, man, thanks for volunteering," Brenton said when we got to his humble home. "Let's hang out again."

I agreed, knowing that he'd be a great buddy to have. What was cool was that he kept it honest. He reached out to me several times over the last couple of weeks. It was time to step up to the plate, embrace his friendship, and start connecting.

CHAPTER 7

Huge Victory

Hey, Anthony. Wassup?" I asked when I saw his name light up my phone. I was sitting in my car outside school on the Friday morning before my first game.

"Somebody's got something big happening tonight," my brother responded. "Go out there and show them, man. Mom and I are coming to the game."

"You don't have to do that, man. I'm sure there's some college party going on at Tech."

"Whatever, my little brother is stepping on the football field for the Lions."

"I might not even get in," I said to him. "Coach has been tripping."

"You'll be suited up, and you will have our support."

Both of us were silent on the phone for a few seconds. It was awkward because we had not had the chance to talk about the fact that I was now only his half-brother. I did not even know if he knew. Though I didn't want to be late for class, I liked the way we had been able to relate to one another.

"Amir, are you all right? Mom told me about everything going on. That's heavy stuff."

"Yeah, I'm cool."

"Well, I love you, man, and nothing's changed with us."

My conversation with my brother meant a lot to me. It got interrupted when Brenton tapped on my car window. I got out and saw several of the football players gathered together ready to walk into the school. They were hyped. I was looking at all of them bouncing up and down, cheering for each other, and I realized that they had a special bond that I wanted to be a part of. Surprisingly, Waxton was with them, but not *with* them. He was real low key and a little off to the side.

I wandered over. "What's up, Wax? You ready to go get 'em?"

He looked up at me and said, "Please, obviously there are still holes in my game. You know it and I know it. If the defenders play me like you played me in practice, I'm messed up."

"Can I give you a piece of advice?" I asked, not wanting my head to be cut off by his smart-aleck comments.

"Yeah, sure. What?" he asked in a humble tone.

"Your eyes always give away the direction in which you're gonna run with the ball. Don't showboat. If you just go for the hole and quit trying to be cool and suave, you're unstoppable."

"You think that's the difference?"

"I know it is," I told him.

Unfortunately, everyone knew we had a gang, the Axes, in our school. As soon as we entered, I could see that the ringleader, Shameek, whom I knew from middle school, had a Glock in his pants and looked like he was about to take somebody out.

Quickly, I stepped over to him and said, "Man, what are you doing?"

Shameek said, "Stay out of this, Amir. I got beef with Blake and Leo. This doesn't concern you."

"If memory serves me correctly, you owe me one, right?" I reminded my old pal.

When he did not have money to go on an eighth grade trip, I got my dad to sponsor him. On the trip Shameek was overwhelmed with emotion and said he never had anybody care enough to help him out like that. He told me that whenever I needed him, he'd owe me one. A few years later I was ready to cash in.

"What do you care about the football team, Amir?"

"I just do, man."

Shameek nodded. He called off his goons and covered the Glock up with his shirt. The team passed by, oblivious to the drama that could have unfolded. At least I thought so.

Leo walked over to me and said, "So Shameek is still upset, huh?"

"Yeah, with you and Blake."

"Dang," Leo said. It was obvious that he didn't want trouble.

"I took care of it."

"For now, but if you know him, then you know he's crazy. This isn't going to be over until someone's dead." I looked at Leo, wishing that he was not telling the truth, but he was. " 'Preciate it."

When we walked past Hallie and her crew of cheerleaders, I told Brenton I would see him later. He headed off in another direction. Seeing the girl got me excited, but I also did not want to let her on to the fact that I was playing ball. I knew she really liked me either way, but I wanted to see how the night was going to go. I needed to see if I got off the bench and made a difference in the game before she knew.

We had a pep rally. It killed me to see all the other cheerleaders flipping except Hallie. I wanted to go out and spot her, but I knew that would only make things worse for both of us. I could only hope that she would find the strength inside herself to do what I knew she could at the game. When our eyes met, she held her head down. I knew she was disappointed in herself. I just wanted to wrap her in my arms and tell her it was going to be okay. However, I stayed seated behind the football team, not wearing my jersey on purpose.

When the school day was over and the pep rally was through, we were eating a pre-game meal. Coach Strong stood before us and said, "Listen, I studied the film of the Tigers and truly believe the only way that we can get beat is if we beat ourselves. You guys are special athletes. Play like it. Remember your assignments. Don't make stupid mistakes, and play your heart out."

I raised my hand. "Amir, you want to say something?"

I stood and said, "Yeah, Coach, I just wanted to follow up with what you said. I've been out here for a couple of weeks, and I thought it was all about x's and o's, but I've learned it's also about the Jims and Joes. You guys care about each other. I want to be a part of the brotherhood."

Waxton stood up and said, "You're in."

Leo stood and said, "That's right."

Blake replied, "Let's go Lions! That's what I'm talking about."

Brenton, who was seated beside me, patted me on the back. Other players came up and gave me dap. We were a team and I was part of it.

That evening when the game was going on, I was actually happy that Coach allowed Colby to start. It really was his position to lose. Unfortunately, he was getting beat on assignments.

He went over to Coach and said, "Put Amir in."

"Your time to shine, baby," Brenton said while we ran to position on the field.

On my first defensive play, the ball was thrown to my side. I guess since they had no film on me their coach thought where I stood was the weak side. I proved his theory wrong. I was the strong side when I stepped in front of the receiver, got the interception, and ran in for a touchdown. The crowd went wild. Hearing my name called over the loudspeaker made me feel real good inside.

When I came over to the sidelines and saw my mom and brother sitting in the stands, waving uncontrollably, I felt even prouder. My heart skipped a few extra beats when I saw Hallie with her hands clutched to her heart. She was searching the sidelines. However, she could not find me. I had on a helmet and blended in with the other players. I saw she was happy though. That let me know she really cared.

We were going back out there on defense since I scored. I watched the quarterback's eyes and felt he was going to throw the ball on the other side. I covered my man like Coach wanted me to. However, the ball was thrown in the opposite direction. I made it across the field to intercept that ball as well. The game was changing and the momentum was swinging our way.

I did not get a touchdown, but we put the offense on the field. Blake threw a pass to Landon. A TD was caught in the end zone.

The score before halftime was tied. But the game was not won. We had a whole other half to play, but the brotherhood I wanted to be a part of was exhilarated. I felt like together we could conquer anything. I was a part of the team and it felt good.

It was halftime of the first game that I had played since the seventh grade. Though things were going right in my world, I jogged off the field and passed a somber Hallie. I stopped and grabbed her hand. At first she did not know it was me because of the helmet. Then I took it off and she recognized me immediately

When our eyes connected, I said, "You *can* do this."

I was straggling at the back of the pack of football players going into the field house so I could see her do her thing. She was the last cheerleader because they call them alphabetically. As her name was announced, I saw the dejection in her face. When she did not reach her goal, instinctively I wanted to go up to her, kiss her, hug her, and tell her everything was going to be okay. However, the only people left on the field in the football program were the coaches. I could hide no more among the guys in pads. I could only hope that she would not be too hard on herself and know that as soon as this game was over, I'd find her, embrace her, and let her know that she would get it the next game.

"Son, you're so good," my mom said to me. Coach nodded to let me know that I had a second to talk with my family.

"Two picks on your first two plays, little brother, for real you got skills," Anthony said.

The three of us stood there for a second. Though we were outside, it felt like we were in a closed box, and there was an elephant in the room that we were not dealing with. That was the fact that my father was absent. Though it had only been a few days, he still had not been home. While my mom seemed happy he left instead of me, I knew she loved her husband. It was not fair that I was the reason they were apart.

"All right, Knight, let's get on in here," Coach said, pointing to the field house. "Your mama can baby you a little later on."

I hugged my mom. Coach pulled my jersey and we headed into the locker room. He immediately got in the middle of the team.

"All right, men, gather around. We're in a war. They want a victory, but we want it more," Coach yelled. "Dial it up! I don't know how the Tigers practice, but I know the Lions have been relentless. We've got the twelfth man on our side. This is a home game, and we need to win it. Let's go show them who has the loudest roar. Remember men, this isn't just about playing right under the Friday night lights. No, this is about character building. You may be tired, but if you hold on, play even harder, and push through the pain, these are the lessons that will carry you through life and make you stronger."

We were all jacked up. We went out in the second half and showed out. The Tigers did not score another point. We scored four more touchdowns and won 42–14.

"That's what I'm talking about," Leo said, lifting me in the air after the game. "Defense shut them down second half, led by my boy Amir Knight."

"Nah, partner, put me down. This was a team effort, for real. What you have … two sacks?"

"Three," he stated humbly.

I asked, "Brenton, how many tackles you have second half? Ten?"

"Twelve," Brenton said, nodding that this was a true team effort.

The guys were getting ready for the after party in the gym. I could not get dressed fast enough because I wanted to see Hallie. My boys wanted me to hang out with them, but as soon as I spotted that beautiful face across the gym, I made my way over there.

"Amir, can I talk to you for a second?" the familiar and usually scary voice calmly said.

I turned and was surprised to see Lexus. She had on long sleeves so I could not see her wrists all bandaged up. I knew she had not been at school since the incident.

"I'm okay … I'm okay," she said, noticing I was taken aback. "I wanted to let you know that I learned a hard lesson. My mom is getting me help."

"That's good."

"I know you really like that Hallie girl. I think you should be with her," she said, like I needed her permission.

"I want you to be okay. I think you're a great girl."

"Yeah, and I don't need to think a guy can control my life."

"Exactly. So you good?" I said to her, not wanting to hold too long of a conversation.

She nodded. "Yeah, it's time I started taking care of me. I'm letting you go."

I nodded again. I did not want to give her a hug and make her get the wrong idea. I could only hope and pray that Lexus was going to truly be okay. I let out a sigh of relief as we went our separate ways.

"Let's dance," I said to Hallie after I asked her friends if I could steal her away.

Hallie was all smiles as she took my hand. Having her in my arms felt real good. She smelled so good and looked so fine. And it was clear that she was into me.

When the fast music came on, I asked her if we could go somewhere and talk. I just laid my head on her chest and told her the situation about my father. She held me for a minute and that felt even better.

"Enough about me," I said. "What's going on with you? You could've flipped out there tonight. I know you wanted to. What stopped you?"

"Amir, I knew you were mad at me. We weren't talking. You stopped working at the gym, and I guess I just lost my tumbling. I need your help."

"You don't. You can do this. But I'm here," I said to her. "What's going on with your mom?" I asked. "I haven't stopped thinking about that."

She looked up, "Honestly, things are looking up. My dad and I went and found her. We put her in a rehabilitation center. She's got a chance, Amir. Thanks to you helping him see how I was serious about wanting to be there for my mom, she's got a chance. Now it's up to her."

"That's awesome news."

"So what about your dad? How do you feel about all of that?" she asked.

"I don't know. I'm just trying not to be bitter about it, you know? I've learned if you let go of the anger and work on your dreams and stop hating, life can work out. What about me and you? Can we work out?" I said to her.

She leaned in and allowed her lips to meet mine. I guess the answer was yes. It was a big deal to have a girl I liked care about me. Unlike with Lexus, this was real. We could help each other through the craziness of life. I was going to get her flipping, believe that.

"Dang it, Knight, get your head in the game," Coach yelled to me the following week when he pulled me from the lineup after two long bombs were thrown my way and the other team was about to score. "What's gotten into you? What's going on with you?"

I could only look into the stands. My brother and mom told me they were not coming to this game. It was in Columbus, Georgia, and that was over an hour away. However, when I ran out in the beginning of the game, fired up to have a repeat of last week's dominating performance, I glanced at the stands and froze when I saw my dad. Just his being there was truly affecting my execution, and not in a positive way I might add.

What was he trying to do? Drag me home? Had my mom not told him that she agreed to let me play? Whatever his reasoning was, it was not a good one because he was standing in the bleachers, frowning. He had my mind all messed up. I wanted to be able to show him I did not need him in my life whether he wanted me to think of him as my father or not. But my heart had a mind of its own.

"You got me putting scared little Colby back in the game. You know we need to win this game," Coach vented on the sidelines. "You got to get your head in this, man."

I was still not looking at him. I was looking past him into the stands, and I guess he looked over his shoulder, recognized my father, and left me alone. When there was a time-out, I heard someone trying to get my attention. I looked over and saw Hallie whistling badly.

"It's the game. You know I can't talk," I said.

"I know. I just want to tell you to hang in there. I saw you miss a couple balls. The guy was able to—"

"All right, I don't need a replay of the game," I said, cutting her off.

"I'm nervous to tumble. I know you helped me some this week, but …"

"It's one minute before halftime. You can do it. Trust your training."

"Seems like you need to take your own advice," she said. She hit my shoulder pad hard—keeping it real—making me appreciate her more before she jogged back over to her team.

Halftime came quickly. The other team led by seven points. I let everyone pass me by and go into the visitors' locker room. I stayed a second to watch the cheerleaders.

I knew I liked Hallie, but when I saw her tumble and do two handsprings in a row and then end it with a full, I think I loved her. I was so proud. I wanted to run out on the field, twirl her around, and scream. Of course, I was too cool to do that, but I was real proud of her.

When I got into the locker room, Coach was not talking to the rest of the team. He was looking for me. I felt bad because I was having a bad performance. Now I was going to get disciplined because I was not following his rules.

"Knight," he said in a forceful tone. "Come here."

"Yes, Coach?"

"I need to talk to you."

"I'm sorry, Coach. This was—"

"No, no, no, follow me. I need to talk to you."

I did not know what was going on at that point. Was my coach going to kick me off of the team? Was he asking me to take off my uniform? Were the few minutes I decided to watch and be a spectator going to cost me my dream of being on his team? When we got to an isolated area, he quit walking and turned around. When he moved out of the way, I was surprised to see my dad.

"I think the two of you guys need to talk," Coach said.

Dr. Knight shook Coach Strong's hand. They exchanged a few words I could not hear. Coach left us.

"What are you doing here?" I said, wanting to cut straight to the chase.

There was no need to warm up. No need to act like we needed to hear the rules. We only needed to get it on with why he was there.

He stepped toward me and said, "Son, I've been doing a lot of thinking. I came here to support you. I know it was wrong the way I acted—to just blurt out the seriousness of our lives and intentionally setting out to hurt you like that. I have been holding in a lot of anger over the years. I don't deserve for you to forgive me, but I love our family. Thankfully I've been off rotation for the last couple of days, because all I can think about is saving my family. Not heart transplants, not saving anyone's life …

"I'm not a part of that," I said, being as truthful as I knew how to be.

"Yes, you are as much my son as Anthony is. There's a saying around the hospital, 'If you feed them long enough, they begin to look like you,' " he tried joking, but I did not laugh. "There has not been a day that you missed a meal. My problem is I wanted you to be *mine* so badly that I never realized you *are* mine. I have been on you to overcompensate for my own shortcomings. You're great in your own right. You had nothing to do with how you got here or who decided to sign your birth certificate. I had a hand in all of those responsibilities. I'm not going to walk away from all of that now. I don't want to walk away from you. If you let me, son, I want to be here for you. I know we only have a little bit of time before you set out on this life and begin your own journey into manhood. I want to do better with you."

I turned around and hit the wall. I could not believe he was saying what I knew I wanted to hear. I loved him so much. I tried so hard to please him, and there he was saying he loved me too.

"I want to move back in the house, son, but I want to know that we can work on us. I want you to be comfortable there. If you got any doubts—"

Cutting him off, I said, "No, no, Dad. Mom misses you. I miss you too."

He extended his arms. I fell into them. We hugged.

"I love you, son. I'm so sorry." He pushed me off and said, "Now get on out there and play some ball, okay?"

Third quarter the coach did not put me in. Another touchdown got away from us. We were most definitely getting burned.

I went over to Coach and said, "I can do this. I'm ready to get in the game."

"Is your head in it?" Coach Strong asked me.

"Yes, sir, because you always told me to trust my training, stay focused on the goal, and dig deep. You helped me clear out some of the cobwebs. My mind is in the game."

"Well, get the heck on out there then. Let's win this thing."

We had one quarter, and we were seventeen points behind. I was on special teams, and I ran one all the way back. We were immediately on defense, and we were three and out. When Blake got the ball back, he led another drive. Just like that, we were only down three points. The clock was not our friend. The home crowd was not on our side either.

When I went back out for defense, it was like the story of my life. So many times people look at what other folks got, and they do not want to stay in their own lane. They do not want to focus on where they want to go. They do not do their assignments. They are so full of rage that they are not free. Free to live. Free to try. Free to dream. Free to be successful, and free to soar. When the quarterback threw the ball in my direction, I caught it and ran it in for a touchdown. The Lions focused on our goals and supported one another. There was no hating, only supporting. That camaraderie led to a huge victory.

STEPHANIE PERRY MOORE is the author of many YA inspirational fiction titles, including the *Payton Skky* series, the *Laurel Shadrach* series, the *Perry Skky Jr.* series, the *Yasmin Peace* series, the *Faith Thomas Novelzine* series, the *Carmen Browne* series, the *Morgan Love* series, and the *Beta Gamma Pi* series. Mrs. Moore speaks with young people across the country, encouraging them to achieve every attainable dream. She currently lives in the greater Atlanta area with her husband, Derrick, and their three children. Visit her website at www.stephanieperrymoore.com.

DERRICK MOORE is a former NFL running back and currently the developmental coach for the Georgia Institute of Technology. He is also the author of *The Great Adventure* and *It's Possible: Turning Your Dreams into Reality*. Mr. Moore is a motivational speaker and shares with audiences everywhere how to climb the mountain in their lives and not stop until they have reached the top. He and his wife, Stephanie, have co-authored the *Alec London* series. Visit his website at www.derrickmoorespeaking.com.

STEPHANIE PERRY MOORE is the author of many YA inspirational fiction titles, including the *Payton Skky* series, the *Laurel Shadrach* series, the *Perry Skky Jr.* series, the *Yasmin Peace* series, the *Faith Thomas Novelzine* series, the *Carmen Browne* series, the *Morgan Love* series, and the *Beta Gamma Pi* series. Mrs. Moore speaks with young people across the country, encouraging them to achieve every attainable dream. She currently lives in the greater Atlanta area with her husband, Derrick, and their three children. Visit her website at www.stephanieperrymoore.com.

WANT A DIFFERENT
point of view?

JUST *flip* THE BOOK!

WANT A DIFFERENT
point of view?

JUST *flip* THE BOOK!

LOCKWOOD LIONS

The Lockwood High cheer squad has it *all*—sass, looks, and all the right moves. But everything isn't always as perfect as it seems. Because where there's cheer, there's drama. And then there's the ballers—hot, tough, and on point. But what's going to win out—life's pressures or their NFL dreams?

HALLIE CHEER Drama

Hallie Ray is jealous of her BFFs.
And sometimes jealousy can ruin everything...

KEEP JUMPING

Stephanie Perry Moore

SADDLEBACK
EDUCATIONAL PUBLISHING

CHEER DRAMA

Always Upbeat

Keep Jumping

Yell Out

Settle Down

Shake It

SADDLEBACK
EDUCATIONAL PUBLISHING
www.sdlback.com

ISBN-13: 978-1-61651-885-1
ISBN-10: 1-61651-885-5
eBook: 978-1-61247-619-3

Printed in Guangzhou, China
0712/CA21201000

16 15 14 13 12   1 2 3 4 5

To Michele Clark Jenkins

You're the best attorney in the world. I so appreciate you always embracing my ideas, putting my vision down on paper, and bringing my goals to life. We have been blessed to co-edit a couple of projects that were written to inspire people to be real and have faith. May every reader learn to not stop dreaming and continue on as you have always told me to do.

Remain a mover and shaker … I love you!

ACKNOWLEDGEMENTS

It is difficult to continue running a race when you feel like you are losing. You may ask yourself why try and cross the finish line when the prize seems to be taken. You look over and others are going faster. They seem stronger and seem to have it all.

The grass may seem greener on the other side of the fence, but trust me, your grass has it going on too. And if you spend more time running your race versus looking over your shoulder, you'd get a faster time. If you spend more time watering your grass, yours will be the nicest on the block. The point here is simple ... keep moving. Don't waste time worrying about others. Fix your weaknesses and operate in your strengths. If you stay in your lane, you'll win your fair share of prizes in life.

Here is a gigantic thank you to the people who are helping me move on to accomplish great things.

Acknowledgements

For my parents, Dr. Franklin and Shirley Perry Sr., thanks for your provisions that keep me going.

For my publisher, especially, Arianne McHugh, thanks for your eagerness to work with me and for the chance to keep me writing.

For my extended family: brother, Dennis Perry, godmother, Majorie Kimbrough, mother-in-law, Ann Redding, brother-in-Christ, Jay Spencer, and goddaughter, Danielle Lynn, thanks for your support. You keep me inspired.

For my assistants: Alyxandra Pinkston and Joy Spencer, thanks ladies for hanging in there, keeping me on point.

For my friends who are dear to my heart: Lakeba Williams, Leslie Perry, Sarah Lundy, Jenell Clark, Nicole Smith, Jackie Dixon, Torian Colon, Loni Perriman, Kim Forest, Vickie Davis, Kim Monroe, Jamell Meeks, Michele Jenkins, Lois Barney, Veronica Evans, Laurie Weaver, Taiwanna Brown-Bolds, Matosha Glover, Yolanda Rodgers-Howsie, Dayna Fleming, Denise Gilmore, and Deborah Bradley, thanks for your love, which keeps me grounded.

For my teens: Dustyn, Sydni, and Sheldyn, thanks for loving your mom. You keep me hungry.

For my husband, Derrick, thanks for being my partner in life who keeps me passionate.

For my new readers, thanks for reading my work. You keep me humbled.

And my Lord and Savior, thanks for allowing me to connect with Saddleback Educational Publishing and help others grasp a love for reading. You keep me blessed.

CHAPTER 1

Looking In

Have you ever felt like your world was perfect? Like it could not get any better? Like you were right where you needed to be, and you hoped nothing would change? You know that feeling of excitement when your heart starts racing and your insides get all gushy because you can't even believe you're experiencing sheer happiness? For some the excitement might come from getting straight As. Others might get a thrill behind the wheel of a new car. Some hearts might race in the arms of a new boyfriend. Well, for me it was being a cheerleader.

Yep, I had longed to sport the precious white uniform with purple and gold accents. I had dreamed of becoming a cheerleader and yelling on the sidelines for my school for years. I had no words to describe what it felt like living my dream.

We cheered, "Go Lions! Go Lions! Beat the Bulldogs! Beat the Bulldogs! Come on, you can do it! Let's go, put your mind to it! Go Lions! Go Lions! Beat the Bulldogs! Beat the Bulldogs! Yay!"

"Hallie Ray, you got this, girl!" Charli came over to me and said. She gave me a big hug between cheers to motivate me.

Charli Black was one of my best friends and the team captain. When Charli tells you you're good, well, that's major. She was the best cheerleader I knew. I mean, if you looked up the definition of cheerleader in the dictionary, her picture would be right there.

"You think I did okay?" I said to her. I was anxious to do a super job.

"Don't get that head all blown up," said feisty Eva. She was my one girlfriend who had no problem speaking out without thinking first. "Just playing. You know you're showing out. Don't slack in the second half."

Eva was a sassy something, but I loved the fact that she said what was in her heart and on her mind. She never tried to sugarcoat her opinion or make the medicine of her words go down easier. She just said whatever came to her. You had to deal with it. Even though her coarse joking got on my nerves sometimes, I really appreciated that she thought I was doing well.

Eva had a twin sister, Ella, who was also on the cheerleading squad. Though they looked exactly alike, their personalities were completely different. Ella was a sweetheart. Though she also said what she felt, she took time making sure that she never hurt anyone's feelings. She really cared about pleasing everyone, whereas her sister couldn't care less if she didn't please a soul.

The last of our crew was Randal. She simply gave me a high-five. She was really shy, but when it was time to cheer, she turned on the magic.

We were all juniors at Lockwood High School, and at this very moment we were performing at our first home football game. Our team was supposed to be dynamic, and as I looked up at the probably ten thousand fans at our sold-out game, I felt pressured to hold my own.

I went up to Charli and said, "Could you please just call the cheers we've been practicing a lot and not the ones you just taught us this week? Please, because I don't want to look stupid."

"I got you, girl," she said to me, as she went on to call out the next cheer.

Charli was on cloud nine. She had gone through a lot of boy drama. Blake Strong, the hottest stud in our school and the quarterback of the team, was her man for the last two years. However, he started tripping and ended up getting with this other girl who gave it up. It broke Charli's heart. She's so beautiful and sweet. Incredibly, Blake's cousin Brenton, who is also a football player, showed up to wipe away her tears.

If being a cheerleader was measured by the heart you had for the sport, then I would have all that I needed. However, that was not the case; you also needed skills. In addition to wanting it really bad, I had a big mouth. That was a good thing when it came to cheering. My problem was that my jumps were lousy. I also had difficulty remembering new cheers and dance routines. Worse than anything, I could not tumble at all.

It was halftime and the score was 14–0. Unfortunately, the score was not in our favor. The crowd booed the team when they went into the locker room. Now it was time to go to the middle of the field and pump up the crowd. With our dance number, we did just that. We were not just a squad who cheered for the football team. No, we were competition cheerleaders too, getting ready to compete for the state championship.

When it was time to announce the individuals on our squad, I wanted to go run and hide. Everyone ran and performed two round-offs, a back handspring, and a tuck. Well, everyone but me. I could barely do a cartwheel much less any major tumbling.

There were twenty girls on our team and watching one after the other after the other tumble on the turf, I was embarrassed. I wished I had their skills. I wished I had their poise. I wished I could do what they could do, but I could not. When my name was called, I did a pitiful cartwheel.

I heard someone out in the crowd yell, "Flip!"

I dashed off the field. There were still a couple more cheers that we were going to do, but I fled. I saw our cheer coach, Coach Woods, give me an unhappy glare. I defied that hard look and went over to the concession stand to get away from the feelings of inadequacy. I bumped into my father.

"You did good, girl. Why did you leave the field? The other cheerleaders aren't finished," he remarked.

I wanted to say, "Isn't it obvious, Dad? I really don't have what it takes to be a level four cheerleader." Level four was reserved for a cheerleader with an amazing tumbling ability that I just did not have.

"Well, are you going to spend the night at Charli's?" he asked. I nodded yes. "All right, well, I'm going to go on home. I just wanted to come out and see my baby girl perform at her first game. You're amazing. No need to rush home tomorrow. Just be smart. Again, baby girl, great job."

I knew he was supposed to say that. I let him kiss my forehead, slip a few dollars in my hand, and feel proud. How the day went from my happiest moment to my most embarrassing one, I will never know. But it happened, and I was dejected. The last thing I wanted to do was get back out on the field and cheer.

I was hungry, so I took the money my dad gave me and stayed in line to get some fries. I didn't want to eat too much and get sick, but since I was not bouncing and flipping all over the place, what difference would it make?

Then a masculine voice that I did not recognize said from behind me, "You really shouldn't be so hard on yourself. They're not doing anything you can't do."

I turned around and my eyes met a guy I had never seen before. My high school was pretty big, but this guy was cute enough that he should have stood out in the crowd. He gave a whole new meaning to the term tall, black, and handsome. His chocolate skin was smooth like a Hershey bar, and he had muscles that I wanted to touch. He looked so built that it seemed like he should be out there on the football field. I quickly turned around, trying to gain my composure.

I knew deep in my soul that I was a talk person. I was taking this test with my friends a few days ago out of a book called *The Five Love Languages of Friendship*, and I realized that I was what the book described as "words of affirmation." That meant words made me feel love, but words could also dramatically tear me down.

Hearing this guy tell me that I could do it was super special and lifted me somewhat. Though he did not know me, he told me what my heart longed to hear. It made me smile, but when I turned back to face him, he was gone.

Did I imagine him? Did I want to hear someone tell me I could do the impossible? After scouting the crowd, looking all over for him, and being unsuccessful, I realized I was dreaming. I needed to wake up because halftime was over and Charli was calling. Whether I liked it or not, I had to cheer.

Strolling into the after party with my girls meant all eyes were on us. Though we were only juniors, we were mad popular. We were five varsity cheerleaders who hung out, and in more than one way, we were thicker than the juiciest steak. We got called meat and a whole bunch of other names when we passed by clusters of guys.

I did not realize my face was glum until Eva said, "Girl, don't be frowning. Ain't nobody going to ask you to dance looking all ugly and stuff. Smile, relax, work your body. Don't let your body work against you. Loosen up."

But it was hard to do that when I saw guys whispering about everyone in my crew but me. They were talking about Ella and Eva's bodies. They were talking about how beautiful Charli was. They were talking about Randal's eyes and hair that flowed down her back. However, nobody was saying anything about Hallie Ray.

All I wanted was for someone to ask me to dance. I was not trying to leave the dance with a guy. I had learned my lesson of being too fast last year.

Maybe wanting attention came because I felt broken. I could blame it on the fact that I was having a ton of problems at home. I was an only child, and my dad was my rock. My mom, however, was a junkie and living who-knows-where. Every day I never really knew whether she was alive or dead. It took me a long time to come to terms with that. I still hoped we could get her clean, get her to change her ways, and get her to want to be my mom more than she wanted to blow on a pipe. Problem was I could not always find her, and my dad was so frustrated trying to get her to do the right thing that he started burying himself in his job working longer hours.

During my sophomore year I had no supervisor at home. So when a senior guy started paying attention to me, I was vulnerable. He said all the things I needed to hear, but he did not mean it. Within the first month of dating me, he had his way. I was no longer pure. He ditched me two months later after he felt that I was all used up. I was devastated and put all my energy into making the team.

I did not want to be used again, but I did not want to be alone at this dance either. When Brenton came up to Charli and she left, it was the four of us. Then a senior came up to Eva. She winked and was gone. When two guys approached Ella, Randal, and me, I knew someone was going to be the odd girl out. I was not surprised when it was me.

"We can stay here with you. We don't have to dance," Randal said, truly meaning it.

"Girl, go have fun," I said with some heart. I didn't want to kill my friends' fun.

Because guys were not into me did not mean I wanted my girls to live my life. Having guys ignoring you and not thinking you were cute enough was not fun. Being passed up hurt.

I could feel other girls in the room hating on me and my friends with their stares. Actually, they were not hating on me because I was in the same boat. The sad thing was that a part of me was envious of what my girls had that I did not: curves, gorgeous eyes, beauty, and popularity with the guys. I was cute but I was not gorgeous, while some of them—even if they didn't think so—were definitely model material. Honestly, I did not even understand why they were my friends. Last year watching the four of them cheer JV while I sat alone in the stands was excruciating. Now I was one of them and still I did not truly feel that I belonged.

Charli walked over to me after one of the songs was over. "Brenton has gone to get me something to drink. Do you want something?"

With attitude I grunted out, "He's *gone* to get you something to drink?"

"I can text him. He told me to ask you if you wanted something. What's eating you?" Charli asked, sensing my tension.

"I'm fine," I muttered.

Charli stood close. "You know I care. So what's wrong with Hallie today? You didn't take your happy pill? You were out there cheering for the first time on the field. I know you had to be excited."

It was not that Charli was so into herself that she did not know what I needed. I could tell she cared. However, she had no clue about the way I cheered during the entire game. The second half was completely different from the way I cheered the first half. After I could not tumble and flip, my excitement faded.

She put her hand on my sassy, short do and said, "Is it the tumbling?" I looked away. "We can work on your tumbling, Hallie. We can work on your jumps. You can get it. You got to get it because we're going to compete in a couple weeks, and we all need to be flipping. We're going to help you. No worries."

I was tired of that phrase. How could she tell me no worries? Easy for her to say because she was the flipping queen. At this point in my life, it was not that I was *unable* to flip. I had a mental block, and I could not convince my mind to let my body fly freely in the air.

"What else is wrong with you, Hallie? I know you, girl. You're sitting here on the wall with your arms folded and your lips poked out. Any guy who wants to come over here will think twice because he won't want to get his head cut off. Eva was right, loosen up."

"You and Eva know nothing about what I'm feeling. You two could have the chicken pox and guys would be attracted to you. Some of us have to work a little harder at it."

"Okay, well, take some advice from us and quit doing the exact opposite of what would make a guy come over here and holler at you, dang. And don't look at twelve o'clock. There's a guy checking you out right now, and he's cute, girl," Charli said, making facial expressions that confirmed what she was saying.

No one who was making her that giddy could be eyeing me. "Don't play."

Charli nodded. "I'm serious."

Then I remembered the mystery man I'd seen at halftime and then thought I'd imagined. Could he be real? Was he there? Nah.

Wanting to believe the possibility, I shared, "There was this one guy earlier today when I was at the concession stand. I turned around, but he was gone. It's like I imagined him."

"Well, I'm not imagining this dude. He's looking at you like you are a biscuit with honey, and he's ready to gobble you up. Turn around slowly, slowly, slowly ..."

When I turned, I quickly turned back to Charli, cutting her off. "That's him! Oh my gosh. That's the fine guy from earlier today!"

I did not have the time to tell Charli to let it be because she motioned him to come over. "Hi, I'm Charli. This is my friend Hallie. Well, I'm going to go get something to drink. See y'all!" she said before leaving. But then she turned and asked, "Uh, what's your name?"

"I'm Amir."

Charli stuck out her hand and shook it. "Hey, Amir. This is Hallie."

"It's you ...," I said to him still stunned.

"Is that a bad thing?"

"No, it's just that I was looking for you earlier before I went back out on the field, and you were gone."

He teased in a pleasant voice, "You were looking for me, huh?"

Stumbling I said, "You ... you said a couple things that were interesting and I just ..."

"I said some things I meant," he said in a serious tone. "You can do all the moves the other girls can do."

I shook my head, having no faith. "Me flipping? Seems impossible."

Confidently he replied, "I work at a gym. I know I can get you tumbling. You should come by and check it out."

I did not say a word, and I could tell he wanted me to accept his invite. His eyes appeared to really want to connect with me—like there was more he wanted to say but didn't.

So I asked gently, "Is there something else?"

"I just don't understand why you don't think you're as cool as your friends. You get all huffed up when they leave. From what I've seen, they ought to be glad to hang out with you. You make their crew look good," Amir said, making my skin tingle.

"Excuse me?" I blushed.

"I didn't stutter. You've got it going on in all the right places, flawless chocolate skin, fly hairdo … no wonder a brother can't keep his eyes off you."

"And what gym did you say you were at?" I asked, knowing I had to see this dude again.

Amir answered, "I didn't, but I'm at Cheer-towne."

Randal and Ella were giggling as they rushed back over to me. They took my attention for a couple seconds, and I wanted to introduce them to Amir, but when I turned around to do so, he was gone. At least this time I knew he was real, and the things he said to me made me look at myself in a different way. Was I selling myself short? Did I have it going on? Was I *all that* too?

I told my father that I was going to spend the night at Charli's house. However, the girls were having so much fun that when I could not find Amir, my new mystery man, I decided it was time for me to take it in. Maybe my dad could watch a movie with me, and I could feel special being his little girl.

When I pulled up, I noticed all the lights were off in my house, but his car was there. It wasn't even eleven, so I hoped he was not asleep. As soon as I opened the door, I heard a whole bunch of breathing, panting, squealing, and kissing. I clutched my chest, hoping that what

I wanted so desperately was coming true. What I hoped to see was my parents back together. It seemed impossible when we had not even heard from my mom. But meeting Amir proved that neat things do happen. I wanted to believe that my mom could just come right back into our lives. She'd get cleaned up and be her beautiful self just like before. My parents would get back together, and my life would be normal again. I guess I was naive.

However, I then heard a lady's voice that I didn't recognize. It was high-pitched and absolutely annoying. I knew I had a loud mouth and got on people's nerves sometimes when I talked, but this woman, whoever she was, sounded screechy. When I flicked on the family room light, I was surprised to see a lady on top of my dad's lap. Neither of them were wearing shirts.

"Oh my gosh, Tim, I thought you said your daughter wasn't coming home tonight!" the stranger said.

I wanted to cut the lights because though the view was not x-rated, it definitely was not appropriate. Not just for me to view, but for my dad to even be engaged in.

"What are you doing?" I screamed. "Who is this lady? Why is she here, Dad? Ew!"

"Tim, you've got to talk to her. You have got to tell her about me. She thinks I'm just some lady," the lady said to my dad, as her eyes watered up.

I heard what she was saying to my dad, and she was insinuating that they had a relationship. That burned me up like I was a pot of water on the stove turned up high. No way was my father involved with her. There was just *no way*.

"Dad, get her out of here! She doesn't belong here," I whined.

"Tim, say something," the lady fussed.

"Okay, Greta, okay," my dad said as he got up. That lady stood behind him, peering at me.

"Hallie, pumpkin, I didn't want to introduce you like this, but this is Greta, my girlfriend."

I just laughed. "Come on, Dad, please. I'd know if you had a girlfriend, okay? Give me a break. Don't try to play it off. We all make mistakes, but she needs to go. Bye, Grits, Grass, or whatever your name is."

The Greta person put on her shirt while she stood on the other side of my dad and explained,

"It's Greta, and I am his girlfriend. Your father and I have been seeing each other for the last six months. I told him I wanted to meet you so it would not happen like this," Greta explained.

"I wasn't ready for all the awkward intros, okay?" my dad said to the lady who claimed to be his girl. "I knew she wasn't ready for this."

"So you think this is better? For her to just walk in and think I'm just some lady. I love you."

"Ew!" I screamed. "Dad!"

The lady reached out her hand to shake mine, but I stepped back.

"I don't want to meet you. I don't even want to know you. I definitely don't want you to be my dad's girlfriend." I went over to the front door and opened it. "Please leave."

My dad came over and quickly shut the door. "Hallie, you don't pay no bills here, dear. You are not kicking anybody out of my house."

"This is our house, Dad. She doesn't live here." I opened the door back up.

He slammed it. "You need to check yourself. I'm trying to ask you to forgive me for keeping Greta a secret from you. Like I said, we've been together for a while and ..."

When my dad got stuck, Greta chimed in, "And things are pretty serious."

"I didn't ask you. And can I talk to my father alone? Goodness, no wonder he didn't want me to meet you. You're real pushy. You have no respect for his relationship with his daughter."

Greta looked at my dad and tears fell. He hugged her. I was literally sick.

"Oh my gosh! I know you are not trying to play on my dad's emotions. He doesn't need a girlfriend, and he definitely does not need a wimpy one."

"Hallie, that's enough. You're being very rude."

"I'm being rude?" I said to my dad, as I started to become emotional. "I'm sitting here trying to talk to my father in my house, and I find him making out with some tramp half his age."

Before I could even blink, my dad's palm smacked my face. I was stunned. The anger and sadness in his eyes hurt my heart. It felt like I had been stabbed. He'd chosen to stand up for some chick, and he looked at me like I had let him down. The stinging on my face paled in comparison to the mental anguish he put me through by slapping me in front of this lady. I did not like her, and I would never forgive him. If I thought I could get away with it, I would slap him back. He looked at me like he wanted me to apologize, and I stared back at him and breathed real hard, basically telling him to hold his doggone breath. As a couple tears fell down my face, he turned to Greta. It looked like she thought he was going to slap me again because she pulled him away.

Though I had lived here with my dad for years, I was the one who felt like a stranger in my own home. My dad was with someone other than my mom, and I felt like I didn't belong. He made me feel like I was no longer important; I became the outsider looking in.

CHAPTER 2

Connection Made

I was frozen like an Arctic block of ice. I could not believe what had just happened. My dad slapped me. I did not deserve that. There's nothing wrong with speaking the truth. He didn't like it, so he hauled off and whacked me across the face.

I was in a trance. I blinked a couple of times, and I started easing back toward the door. I wanted no part of him, which was ironic because he had been my rock for so long. Now it was like someone had suddenly taken a hammer and smashed our relationship. I was not aware that my eyes were puffy and filled with salty tears. I just knew that my vision was blurred and my dad was in another lady's arms versus apologizing to me.

As soon as he heard me fidgeting with the door, his focus shifted, but it was too late. "Hallie, Hallie, I'm so sorry. Please forgive Daddy. I don't know what got in me."

I could not open the door fast enough. I could not get out of my dad's house quick enough. I could not stop replaying that sobering moment.

"Let go of my arm, Dad. Leave me alone. You hit me! How could you?" I screamed.

He cried out, "I'm so sorry, baby. I'm so sorry."

Though his eyes had remorse like I'd never seen before on my father's face, he had severed our connection in a way I could not explain.

"Tim, just let her go," this problem-causing Greta lady said. "Let her go."

As soon as I was no longer in his grip, I turned around, opened the door, and ran out. I fumbled for my keys and overheard their conversation.

"Just give her some time," Greta said, seeming to know she had my dad under her control.

Surprisingly, my dad argued back, "No, I gotta talk to her now. Hallie and I have never had a blowup like this. Just let me talk to my daughter. Please, stay back." To me he said, "Hallie, come back."

I could not get in my car fast enough. I could not pull out of the driveway quick enough. I could not push the gas pedal hard enough. I had to get away—far away—from the two of them.

I knew immediately that I could not go to Charli's or Randal's house because there would be too many questions from the adults. However, Ella and Eva had more freedom. The twins' mom worked at night. Mama B was really cool. She would not even mind if I was over. No questions asked. She would not go calling my dad or anything. She was just one of those moms who would just be happy I was safe. Yup, to Ella and Eva's house I went.

As I drove, I wondered how my father could betray me like that. Not only did he give me a physical slap in the face, but emotionally he beat me up by putting me in that position in the first place. How come I did not know he had a girlfriend? True, cheerleading had consumed me, practicing all the time, hanging out with my girls all summer, but was I *that* naive to what was going on in his world?

When I pulled up to the twins' apartment complex, it did not surprise me to see Eva passionately kissing up on some boy. It always surprised me how drastically different the twins were. Eva dressed a little bit more provocatively, and she liked wearing her hair down. Ella's was mostly pulled back, and there's no way that she'd be kissing anyone, much less just any somebody.

I wanted to talk to both of them because they had such different perspectives. Eva would keep me tough, and Ella would get in the mud and wallow with me. It was good being with the two of them when I had drama. I needed someone to tell me to suck it up but equally important was having someone who understood and allowed me to vent. However, I knew if Eva had a guy with his hands and lips all into her, there was no way she was going to turn around and see what was up in my world. I could only hope Ella was not into some Lifetime movie that had her glued to the television.

"Ella's in there. I'll be back," Eva said without a backwards glance.

Maybe Eva didn't realize how upset I was. I gave her the benefit of the doubt, but who was I fooling? Everyone knew Eva loved being with her flavor of the week more than she loved giving a pep talk.

My problem was not her problem. So I mouthed, "Be careful" and left her to flirt. When her sister answered the door, she was a godsend because she immediately felt my pain.

"What is wrong, baby?" she asked. I fell into her outstretched arms and put my head on her shoulder.

"Oh, Ella, I don't wanna keep going on. Life is too hard," I blurted out.

"That is absolute crazy talk," she said, sounding like her sister. "I wanna hear all about it, but you gotta calm down. We were talking about you after you left the dance, girl. What is your problem? You were pouting all evening, and I know you are not crying because you couldn't do a few flips at the game. You'll get them. We're gonna see to that. We're adding extra practices to help all the girls get everything down. So no sweat."

"I actually wish that was it. I was upset earlier because it was horrible watching y'all flip from the middle of the football field to the parking lot and back. I just stood there watching because I had no ability," I explained, reliving my misery.

Ella moved back from the door so I could enter and huffed, "You're exaggerating."

"I know I'm exaggerating, but that's how I felt," I voiced as I plopped on her couch. I wanted a pity party. I did not want to chill.

Not backing down, she defended, "You wouldn't be on the team if you didn't have any skills."

"All right, Charli Black," I said to Ella.

She went into the kitchen. Leaning my head back, I *so* wished my woes did not exist. Finally I found a guy who seemed to make my heart leap, and I couldn't dive into his arms because my father stripped away my dignity.

"Is it that time of the month? Drink this," Ella said, handing me a cup of hot tea.

"No, it's not that time of the month. Actually, it should be coming. Maybe that is why I've been a little extra moody. I don't know."

"Well, here. Drink it. This will calm you down. Tell me, talk to me. What's going on?"

"It's my dad," I confessed. My friends loved my father, so I knew my dramatic statement would cause an uproar.

"My buddy? I saw him at the game. What's the problem? He's the best," Ella said, having no reason to think he'd cause me grief.

"Yeah, he went to the game and left early. Check this out; I came home, girl, and he's got a squeeze. Some hoochie I have never met and absolutely can't stand. He was making out with her all hot and heavy in the family room. They were practically doing the do right before I walked in."

"You caught him, girl?" Ella said, frowning and chuckling at the same time.

"See, you think this is funny," I said, clearly not happy.

"No, no, I'm just tripping. Your pops? I don't even want to imagine it. Ew."

"Exactly, and he's not even your dad. It was double ew for me."

"Well, you were supposed to spend the night at Charli's."

"He's just a hypocrite," I yelled.

"What do you mean? He's an adult," Ella defended.

"Yeah, but he tells me to save sex until I'm married. Why was he tryna have it? He's not married to that lady. I don't even think he and my mom got a divorce."

"I didn't think he and your mom ever got married. How could they get divorced?" Ella asked.

"The common law stuff applies," I vented, remembering I told my girlfriends way too much.

"Can I just talk to you?" Ella said. " 'Cause you know I love you, right? So if I say anything, it's coming from a good place. I know you like to hear positive things, but sometimes you gotta hear the truth even though it's hard to swallow."

"Talk to me," I said to her, believing I was ready to hear some straight talk.

"Your dad needs to be happy. All he does is fix cars, work all the time, and take care of you. Me and my sister wish we could get my mom somebody. She's working three jobs and has no social life, while our dad's got a brand new family and doesn't even give her the time of day. I don't know if she's still caught on him or not, but I'm saying all this to say her life needs to move on, and if your dad's life is moving on, don't get in the way of his happiness."

I just looked away at that moment. I heard what she was saying, but that wasn't the place I was at. This was my father, the man who was supposed to love me. He should not have love in his heart for some lady who would tell him to give me space in a time of crisis. What the heck? I was so upset this Greta person would say that and not realize that I could wreck my car in the state I was in.

"You don't understand," I finally said to Ella.

"I do understand, Hallie. The thing is all of us do. Me, Charli, Eva, and Randal think you are jealous of other people. The crazy thing is, you have no reason to be. We see you squinting and rolling your eyes, not being happy for us. When we are happy for ourselves, it's like you hate that or something. If you love people, you should love them without conditions. And if you weren't so busy in everybody else's Kool-Aid, you would understand your flavor's sweet enough." I looked away again. "You can respond so we can talk about it, or we can just watch the TV."

She waited for me to respond. I felt like I was unable to breathe much less talk. Ella shrugged her shoulders and threw me a blanket.

When the commercial came on, Ella said, "I love you, but you need to take in what I'm saying. We called you out, girl. We got your number, and you need to work on that."

"Hallie, get up sweetheart," a soothing female voice said to me.

I jumped up, unaware of where I was. I didn't know how long I'd been sleeping. However, I realized all that I had been through with my dad was not a dream. Ms. Blount, Ella and Eva's mom, was standing right over me.

"It's okay, baby, it's just me. Your dad's been looking for you."

"He doesn't care about me. Trust me, Mama B. Please, don't tell him where I am."

"Well, honey, I didn't know he wasn't supposed to know. Us parents of the five musketeers have a close connection because you girls are growing, and we need to have an alliance so we'll always know where you are at all times. So when he called me, I was on my way home, and I was happy to report that your car was here. I don't know everything that's been going on, so I don't know what's got you and him so upset, but

I can tell you this," she said, giving my shoulder a squeeze, "he loves you, and he wants you to come home."

"Do I have to go?" I whispered.

"You know the answer to that. No, you don't. If I say you do have to go, you might go somewhere else you're not ready for. Your father knows that too. He wants you to go home on your terms, but he wants you to know that he's sorry, and that he wants to talk to you. Those are the two things he told me to tell you. As parents, we make mistakes. Again, I'm not trying to go all into detail about what happened with you and your dad, but I know it can't be so bad that you can't forgive him."

"It was bad," I said to her before looking down.

"Have you ever done anything that you needed him to forgive you for?" she asked.

That was a trick question because she knew the answer was yes. I knew where she was going with this. If I had done something wrong before then, I needed to forgive him as he had forgiven me.

Making her job easier, I said, "I got it." I stood with outstretched arms. "I know parents aren't perfect, and I appreciate you admitting that, Mama B, but sometimes y'all do stuff that break us down, and I thought your job was to lift us up."

She put her arms around me and said, "Point taken. For someone to be so wise and make such a profound statement, you can build your own self up. You don't need to look to your dad, friends, or anyone else to give you happiness. Dig way deep down in your soul and find your own path. I'ma need for you to be strong because when your girlfriend, Miss Eva, walks her little butt up in my house, and it's after three o'clock in the morning, she will get down, and she'll need a counselor. I'm sure whatever it was with your dad didn't mess you up the way your girlfriend's about to be jacked."

"Huh," I said huffing, thinking if she only knew.

"Cut your father some slack, catch some sleep here, and I'll tell him you'll be home in the morning. Is that good?"

"Yes, ma'am."

The next day when I pulled up, my dad's car was there. He was usually at his shop early on

Saturday mornings. I did not know what I was going to find. Was Greta there with him? Was he still angry with me? Or did he even care that I was back home? I opened the door and saw him rise up from his recliner. He rushed over to the door, displaying the same remorseful face that I saw last night.

"Hallie, I apologize about last night. I don't wanna keep on saying I'm sorry. I overheated and I crossed the line with you. I know some parents spank, slap, and kick, but that's never been me and you. Oh, look at your face, it's a little puffy. I knew I hit you too hard. I just couldn't believe the things you were saying, and I let my emotions get the best of me. I love you, baby. You are my number one girl. That's never gonna change," he expressed with full emotion.

"Dad, please, don't tell me what you think I wanna hear. I was just with Ella and she was right. Maybe only wanting to hear the good stuff isn't good for me. I'm not ready for you to have a girlfriend. I just have to go on the record and say that. However, I know you need to be happy, and you need to love your life. But I'm simply not ready for that, Dad."

"I know, baby," he said, as he grabbed me and let me cry on his chest. "Don't worry about that. We'll get this figured out. Right now we need to get me and you solid again, get our connection flowing the right way. Tell me you forgive me, baby," he pleaded in a caring tone.

"I'm sorry too, Dad. I forgive you, but I need you to forgive me for being a jerk. I know I pushed all the wrong buttons, but I just thought you and mom—"

He cut me off and said, "Come on, Hallie, not … not that again. Your mom and I are never gonna get back together. Ever. That's over. I don't even know if she's got herself together … I don't know, I just … I don't wanna talk about your mom. I'm not trying to get upset again," he said. "I'm gonna go work on your car, wanna help me?"

"You going to work on my clunker?" I said, knowing it had been on its last legs for a bit.

"Yeah, maybe we can bond, hang out, fix it up. Would you like that?"

"Yes," I said, remembering days when I'd just hang out with my dad at the mechanic shop and be his little assistant.

For us to do that again really meant a lot to me. He walked back over to me, put both of his hands on my face, and said, "I just wanna tell you, I love you so much, and we're gonna continue to talk to each other and not let emotions get out of hand anymore. Okay?"

"Yes, Daddy."

We were bonding, and it was a great thing. I was glad that I didn't seriously think about ending my life. That was yesterday's drama. What a difference a day made! Note to self: a good team keeps playing until the game is over. Life could change in a moment, and it could change for the better; you never know.

My girls really did have a huge influence over me. I took every single word that Ella boldly told me to heart. I needed to quit looking at what other people had that I wanted and figure out a way to better *me* instead. Not only did my dad fix my car and have it riding perfectly, but he gave it a paint job, and he knocked out some of the dents. My ride wasn't brand new like Charli's pretty, black BMW, but it wasn't a dud anymore either. It had a little flare, and I had some confidence that it was not going to break down at any moment.

Already I was moving in the right direction. Being more proud and satisfied, my dad gave me some money to take tumbling lessons so I could try and get the skills I lacked. I was headed to the Cheertowne gym and secretly hoped to see Amir from my school. If he wasn't there, I really hoped there was someone who could teach me what I thought was impossible—how to tumble. I could not believe I had the nerve to try this.

When I pulled up to the gym and saw all of the cars, I lost my nerve. Actually, I started getting antsy. My dad was in his car behind me. He had to follow me over to sign waivers.

After parking and not getting out, he knocked on my window and said, "Let's go in."

I shook my head. He tried to open my car door, but it was locked. The knots in my stomach had grown in size from golf balls to softballs.

"Come on, baby, you can do this. You want me to take the tumbling lessons too? If you don't get outta that car, I will take the lesson and show you that it's no sweat to flip."

The last thing I wanted to do was have my father embarrass me or have people gossip. As I saw a crowd of folks walk inside and stare, I knew they would be able to identify him with me. Because I took too long to think, he headed inside.

I quickly got out and hollered, "Okay, okay, I'm gonna try. I don't want you to pay for a whole month though. I just wanna take one class. Let's just see how that goes because there's no need for me to stay if I can't perform."

When I walked into the gym, it was super crowded. There were a lot of little girls. I could peek into the gym and see so many people tumbling on the wall-to-wall mats and doing their thing. I had to get this, but truly I felt too old to learn. I hated how I was second-guessing myself. When I saw a familiar girl, I exhaled because I was so relieved.

"Hey, you go to my school don't you?" I asked the girl at the counter. My dad was busy filling out papers.

"Yeah, I'm Lexus. I'm a senior at Lockwood High."

Intrigued I asked, "You work here?"

"Yeah, I'm teaching tumbling."

I started biting my nails. It was a really bad habit. With the acrylics my dad had invested in, I had not been biting them lately. However, when I was super nervous and sick to my stomach, my fingers just managed to find a way into my mouth, and there was nothing I could do about it.

"You'll be fine," she said. "Let's get to work."

I started looking around the gym. I knew I was looking for Amir, but I couldn't find him. So I had to try with her.

"You want me to stay?" my dad asked, seeing I was scared.

"No, Dad. That's why I drove my car. You go on ahead and work. You stayed home with me yesterday. You're already behind. I'll see you afterwards. Thanks so much."

"Well, come by the shop when you're done. You know I can't hear the cell ringing," my dad said, "and I wanna hear how the session went." He gave me a peck on the cheek and was gone.

After I warmed up, Lexus and I tried flipping. I watched to see what she was doing, and she expected me to do it, but that wasn't working. When she tried to flip me over, she wasn't strong enough. She wanted me to do a backbend, but that was difficult too. I was so frustrated.

Just when I was about to give up, the place erupted with little girls laughing. Amir had walked into the gym, and all the little girls ran up to him like he was some rock star or something. It was amazing to watch. He bent down and gave them all high-fives. He was really cool with those babies. Not only did Amir know the right things to say, it was apparent he knew what to do. Lexus stopped paying attention to me. Checking him out I saw that he was muscular and quite handsome—even more handsome than I remembered.

"I'll be right back. Keep stretching," she said. She rushed over to the mayhem.

She tried to tell the little tumblers to keep working out, but they didn't wanna work with the other coaches. They wanted to work with Amir. Maybe he had the magic touch? I so wished he'd come over and help me, but I knew that was going to be impossible. I knew I looked awkward in there working out. I sure felt gangly. Then an older gentleman came out and called Lexus into his office, and Amir came over to me.

Amir playfully said, "Hey, so I see you took me up on coming to the gym. You think you can do this, huh?"

"You told me I could. I'm starting to doubt it, but I figured I'd give it a try. Why? Can you help?" I flirted back.

"Yeah, I was coming in today to pick up a check, but I don't mind helping at all. If you're okay with that. Put your hands over your head and bend back."

"We just tried that, and it didn't work."

"I got you, try it," Amir encouraged.

He put his arm underneath my back. "Just go back and put your hands on the mat."

I took a deep breath and bent backwards. Before I knew it, he pushed my hands back a little. I had done it.

"Kick over," he commanded.

That was a joke, but somehow I found the strength and I did it. When he wanted me to flip forward, I thought he was joking, but I tried it and fell, toppling Amir as well. He landed on me and our eyes locked. Our hearts were both racing; I could feel his beating in unison with mine. There was something about

Amir that attracted me, and I could tell he was attracted to me too.

"If you're committed to this, we can get you tumbling. You've got muscles. You want it. You just got to get over your fear, and I think that's gonna come with practice. These mats aren't going to let you hurt yourself. As long as I'm standing here, you'll be fine. Are you in?" His eyes asked the same question and I nodded. "The goal is to have you doing handsprings in a couple of weeks."

"That's impossible," I told him.

"I don't believe in impossible. Whatever it is that I want, I go get."

"Well, I think you better get up before these little kids around here get the wrong idea."

"I'm not getting you all steamed up, am I?"

"Ha-ha-ha," I laughed because of course the answer was yes, but I wasn't about to tell him that.

When we both stood up and he quickly turned away, I could see that his pants started getting a little tight. I realized I was getting him excited too. Yeah, Amir was into me in a way he could not control. We kept practicing and smiling. How cool, a connection made.

CHAPTER 3

Gotta Try

Randal, Ella, and I made our way to the locker room to change for gym class. "Okay, so you got to give us the scoop," Randal said.

I was smiling, but I was not telling. I looked at both of them and just shook my head. I was known as the girl with the big mouth, but ironically I was keeping my mouth closed.

Ella chimed in and said, "Seriously, Hallie, don't even shut us out. Charli said something about some guy you were talking to at the dance. You came over to my house, and you didn't even say anything. Who is the guy?"

"It's nothing like that," I snickered.

"Okay, we'll discuss the details and determine if it's nothing like that. Just tell us everything," Randal demanded.

"Yeah, talk to us. Does the guy play football?" I shook my head and Ella continued. "Does he play basketball?"

I shook my head again. I did not want them to go down the road they were trotting. However, I could not keep them from drilling me.

"Well, is he on the baseball team?" Ella asked.

Randal cut in and said, "Do we even have a baseball team?"

Ella answered, "That's right, no. So he runs track and field."

"I don't think he's in any of those sports," I said to them.

"Is he in the band, drumline, throwing down, or something?" Ella questioned, as she was really trying to put this guy in a group.

I did not realize it, but the questions they were asking were starting to annoy me. I did not know if it was because I thought they were being too nosey or that I did not like their snobby standards. Why did the guy have to be in anything? But deep down I knew I wanted him to be known too.

One of the few memories of my mom was the fact that she loved watching the movies *Grease* and *Grease 2*. There were these two groups: the Pink Ladies and the T-birds. They could not date just anybody. They had to date somebody within their own clique because they had a rep to protect. I guess I had an ideal guy in my mind that I was looking for. Not only did I want him to be handsome, charming, and into me, but I also wanted him to be popular. I was too quick to understand that Amir was not in the in crowd.

"Okay, so this guy isn't in anything. Hopefully he's smart," Ella said, trying not to say that he's a loser.

I shrugged my shoulders because I had no clue. It was not like I asked him for his résumé and report card. When I thought about being with him at Cheertowne, I knew he may not have any of the usual tags we females deem as prime dating material, but he definitely had swag.

"I told y'all there's nothing to tell. It's just a guy I talked to a couple of times. He works at a gym. It's no big deal," I uttered, trying to get them off my back.

"A guy who works at a gym?" Ella teased. "I don't know about that one, and you know I always have something good to say. That's a little suspect. He wasn't fruity-acting was he?"

"See, why it got to be all that? Why you got to go there?" I said, wanting to defend my new friend. "It's no big deal."

I slammed my locker shut. They knew when it came to friends that I didn't discriminate. They also knew I'd never like a guy who didn't like girls. Why were they pushing me? Needing distance from my girls, I went to wash my hands. I bumped into Lexus from Cheertowne and my eyes widened, knowing she heard my conversation.

"Hey," I said to her, trying to play it off. "I didn't know you were in this class. I didn't know seniors had to take it."

Coldly, she said, "Not that I owe you an explanation, but I need it to graduate, so I'm taking it now. Excuse me."

"Lexus, it's me, Hallie, from the gym. Why you acting like that?" I asked. I was confused by her tone.

Lexus rolled her neck and eyes at me and said, "I don't know, maybe because cheerleaders get on my nerves. I heard you dissing my friend like it's no big deal to call him practically gay and stuff. And to think I thought you were cool. Amir thinks you're cool."

"I wasn't trying to be disrespectful. I didn't say anything bad about him or anything."

"Of course not. But did you straighten out your girls? And I could tell from your voice that you felt that because he wasn't a jock, Amir was not worth telling your girls about. I wonder if he'll think it's cool that you think so little of him," she said. She scurried around me, bumping my shoulder as she exited the locker room.

"Wait. Where you going? Let me explain," I said as I opened the locker room door.

I did a double take as I saw Lexus rush up to Amir. When he saw me, he smiled and waved. I was so embarrassed. I turned around quickly and tried to go back in the locker room, but I could not get the door open. I tried pushing the door, but Randal and Ella were pushing from the inside.

"What'd you forget? Turn around or we'll be late," Randal said. "You know Coach Woods wants us to set an example as cheerleaders and not be tardy for her class."

"That's the guy, y'all," I said. I was too nervous to turn around.

Ella got excited and asked, "Where? Who is he? The way you ran off, we knew you liked him."

"You don't know him, okay? But ..." I paused and motioned my head in the direction that Amir and Lexus were standing. "He's talking to that girl over there."

"The one who's pointing at us?" Randal said, taken aback.

"Looks like he's already taken," Ella remarked, not realizing that she was unveiling to me why Lexus was tripping out.

That's when it dawned on me. How ditsy was I? Lexus was salty with me because she liked Amir, and when we were at Cheertowne, she saw our connection too. Who knew what she was telling him? Had I thrown him under the bus by not defending him to my friends? Was I truly embarrassed that he was not a jock?

When Amir walked away and did not come over to me, I knew I messed up. Amir was walking over to Coach Strong's side of the gym. I was able to exhale a little bit because that meant he was not actually in my gym class but just had gym during the same period. Not knowing what I was going to say to him, I knew I needed to say something. He was a big deal to me. I had only known him for a short time. I met him on Friday night and this was Monday morning. Though my world had been a little crazy over the weekend, he was a bright spot in it, and I had to fix things.

"Hey you!" I said to him.

"What's up?" Amir replied quickly, waiting for me to say something more. "Anything else?"

Going into damage control, I said, "Lexus was in the locker room, and it appears she thinks I'm too stuck up."

With reason and control, he simply asked, "Are you? Do you think I'm not worth the time of day because I'm not an athlete for our school?"

I did not how to answer that. I did not want to lie to him, and I did not want to hurt his feelings either. I did not want to appear shallow, but what was wrong with standards? Thankfully, Coach Strong blew his whistle and called his class over to him. I did not have to say anything.

Before Amir left, he touched my hand and said, "Just so you know, I have my own mind. I get to know people for myself. Folks don't sway me, particularly ones with their own agenda. So don't sweat my conversation with Lexus, though it's nice to know you care."

When he walked off, Ella came over with Randal following and said, "He is a hottie."

"Yeah, you need to try to get to know him," Randal replied.

During the class period, we had to go outside and play flag football. For Amir not to be an athlete, he was pretty dominant, catching both the good balls that were thrown his way and the bad passes that were not thrown as elegantly. When he was on the defense, he was even more stellar, taking the ball away from the intended receiver. Coach Strong stopped watching, pulled Amir out, and stood on the side of the field talking to him for the last fifteen minutes of class. I was so nosey that I almost ran over to eavesdrop.

"Why don't you tell him the truth that you're not really interested?" Lexus snuck up behind me and challenged.

"You don't even know me," I said to her. "You don't know what I'm interested in."

"No, but I heard you talking. He won't believe me … you should tell him that unless he has a varsity letter you're not interested."

Tired of the games, I said, "Maybe you should tell him that you are interested."

"Maybe I will," she said before jetting away.

I actually did not know why I had to be at the mother-daughter cheerleader tea. I did not have a mother who was consistently present in my life. I tried to get Coach Woods to exempt me from being there, but the strong-willed lady insisted. Charli's mom was kind enough to allow me to sit with them, and it did not look so awkward because Ella and Eva were two girls with one lady as well. Though I was with Charli and Mrs. Black and did not look so out of place, I still felt uneasy.

We were in the teachers' dining hall. The tables were beautifully decorated. Whitney, our co-captain and an obnoxious senior, was also sitting at our table. She wanted to be captain badly, but thankfully Charli beat her out. Seeing her mother, who did not appear pleased by the choice of the catered meal, let me know Whitney did not fall to far from the tree.

Whitney leaned in and whispered, "Guess your mom couldn't come, huh? Oh wait, that's right ... you don't live with your mom."

I could not tell if she was saying this to deliberately hurt me, but I did know that she had been giving me the eye during practice, like I was not holding up my end. I could get that. I could not flip and everybody else on the team could. Yeah, yeah, yeah, I could give her a pass on that, but she did not have to put me down or state the obvious.

Whitney's mom rudely asked, "Both of these girls aren't yours, are they?"

Mrs. Black said, "Pretty much, yes!"

I could have hugged her, not because I wanted her to lie, but for the fact that she claimed me. She reached over and hugged me. I saw her heart and knew she did not want me to be an outsider. I was truly touched.

She winked at me and went on to explain. "This is my daughter, Charli, and her best friend, Hallie, who's pretty much like a daughter to me."

"Oh," the woman paused. "I see. Hallie, your mother was working today?"

This lady did not know me. I detested when adults did that. It was uncomfortable. First off, if I did not offer any information about my mom, do not go asking me. I knew she was the adult, but being rude was wrong. What if my mom was deceased? She would have been embarrassed by her tone if I had said my mom was dead. I was so frustrated that I just forgot protocol.

Overcome with emotion, I said, "My mom's strung out on drugs and couldn't be here, okay. Are you happy?"

I threw my napkin down and left the table. I could not get to the women's restroom fast enough. Actually, if I would have had any wits about me, I would have grabbed my purse and keys and headed out the door instead of to an isolated stall. I did not want anybody to bug me; I just wanted to be alone in my misery.

I was not in this position because I had done something wrong. It was my mother's own poor choices that left me half orphaned if there even was such a term. I knew it could be worse. My dad could have abandoned me too. I could not imagine how it felt to not have any parents want you, love you, raise you, and be there for you. But at my school I knew my situation was not unique. Suddenly the bathroom door opened, and Eva barged in yelling without discretion.

Eva barked, "Where are you, girl? Don't be tripping about not having no mom. You know my dad ran out on us. So wassup?"

Upset, I said, "But your mom is here right now, so just go back out there and leave me alone."

Eva said, "Well, I'm not in here alone."

"Yeah, she's not alone," Ella said in a caring voice.

"Come on out. Please come talk to us," Randal pleaded.

"My mom is giving Whitney's mom a piece of her mind right now, so you need to come on back out to the table and not let anybody run you away," said Charli.

"I love you guys, I do, and I can't imagine what it's like not to have a dad there to tell you you're beautiful and provide for you and do all the stuff dads are supposed to do because my dad is there. But unless you've walked in my shoes, you don't know how I feel. Coming to a mother-daughter tea and knowing that your mom would rather have her mouth on a bong than on a fork is harsh. She'd rather lose her mind than stay sane and raise a daughter. She chose to walk away rather than be a part of her daughter's life and take the good with the bad. To be rejected that way by the lady who carried you for nine months and brought you into this world is something unexplainable."

"Come out of there, please," Charli said as she shook the stall door.

I wanted to snap my fingers and be home. That wasn't realistic. Knowing I had to move on, I opened it.

"Go wash your hands," Eva turned up her nose and teased.

"I didn't even use the bathroom," I said to her.

Eva grunted, "So? You in there."

The crazy chick turned on the sink for me. They all laughed. Finally I started laughing too and I cried. It was that time of the month, and I was sick of being so emotional. I tried to get it all out.

"I'm sorry you're hurting," Randal said, giving me a hug.

"Thanks, I'm just trying not to be envious of what you guys have. Ella called me out on it the other night."

Ella said, "I did, but it's understandable that you want a mom."

"I know, but I don't want to be mad at you guys because you have moms."

"Well, you're not mad at us, are you?" Eva said. "I don't get upset because you have a dad who buys you a car, fixes it, and drives around all night when he doesn't know where you are. Girl, my dad couldn't care less."

I said, "I know, everybody's situation is different."

"Everybody's situation isn't what it appears either," Charli said.

We all looked at her like, *Uh, like you have any problems*. And she looked back at us like, *Yeah, I do*. I was not prepared for what she was going to share.

I was blown away like a measly leaf caught up in a wild wind storm when she said, "My dad's been cheating on my mom. I think they're going to work it out, but I caught him going out with some other lady."

I glanced sideways at Ella. "Did you tell her what happened to me?" I asked.

Ella boldly said, "No. It's not the same, Hallie."

"What happened to you?" Charli asked.

I said, "I caught my dad pretty close to doing it with some other lady."

"Yeah, but your dad's not married. Imagine how I felt seeing my father parading out and about with some strange woman, like he has no wife. I mean, gross. My parents are separated right now."

"Your mom is so strong. I would have never known," I said, realizing I wasn't the only one with drama.

Charli lectured, "And don't y'all say anything!"

"We won't. We won't!" Randal said, shaking her head.

"I just wish life was easy. That things were all right and parents did what they're supposed to do. I worry about my mom. I don't know where she is. She could be dead, and I wouldn't even know. It's killing me," I confessed.

"Maybe you should try to find her," Charli said.

"Yeah, it's like I was telling you," Ella piped in. "If you don't like your situation, try and change it. We'll help you look if you want."

"The places my mom hangs ... I never want you guys to be there. Besides I don't know where to begin. It's not that simple," I said to them.

"But you gotta try," Randal said.

"You wouldn't be my girl if you didn't go and look for your mom," Eva added.

I nodded. I so appreciated them for getting up from their comfortable place to come be with me in my difficult moment. How could I be jealous of such precious souls? They gave our friendship everything. I needed to take in their words and try and find my mom so I could at least know what was up with her. To be the best me I could be also meant that I could be the best friend that they deserved in return. They were right; I had to look forward. I just had to.

"So would you like to go out and celebrate your progress?" Amir said to me after our fourth session together.

I was super excited. First, because I had done a flip on my own. Second, because we were connecting. The fact that Amir wanted to take me out made my heart go pitter patter.

"I still can't believe I was tumbling," I said to him a little later on when we sat in McDonald's eating Big Macs, fries, and drinking smoothies that Amir had purchased.

"I knew you could do it. You had what's called a mental block. You had the skills and the capability to tumble, but you just wouldn't throw it. Don't retreat on me. Let's build to make the flips on point."

Thinking back to a nightmare time, I said, "Yeah, I learned it a long time ago, but I think I fell on my head or something, and I just never wanted to do it again."

"But now you got it." Amir stroked my hand.

"Yeah, when you stand there. What am I going to do when you're not around? If you are not going to be there, I don't think I can do it."

"Don't talk negative, Hallie. Believe in yourself, fly girl," he said, looking at me like I was the delicious Big Mac. "Those girls on your team have nothing on you."

"Come on, Amir, please. Seriously, have you seen my crew?"

"Yeah, and I wonder sometimes why you hang out with them. You know, you make them look better."

Amir was too good to be true. He thought I was worthy of praise. I was elated he saw me as a jewel.

But being serious, I said, "My friends are beautiful."

"And so are you," he soothed. He touched my cheek. "I care about you, Hallie. I'll never forget seeing you on the football field last week. You were the most exuberate one. You had fire. You wanted to be out there. Not just to look pretty, but to support the team."

"So I didn't look pretty?" I said, messing with him. I winked and took a gulp of my strawberry-banana smoothie.

"I already spoke on that," he said. He had me blushing.

"Why did you come up and talk to me when I was at the concession stand? I mean, we never met. You didn't even really say hi. You just made a nice comment and was out."

" 'Cause I saw a girl with so much potential and fire, and it was like someone took water and doused your flames as soon as you went onto the field at halftime. Everyone on the team was flipping but you. Anyone could clearly see you were dejected. You fill out your uniform nicely. You can tell in your arms you got muscles. Your legs are toned. I knew you could flip. That's what I do, teach people how to tumble, jump up in the air, and just go for it. I guess I wanted to encourage you."

"And I thought it was impossible for me to do it, and you came along and made it work for me," I said with gratitude.

"Exactly. So when you get out there Friday night and it's time to tumble, show out. I'm sure your parents will be up there rooting for you and all that."

Why did he have to say that? I hung my head low. I was not ready to think of tumbling under the lights. And I could only wish I did not long for my mom to show up. Knowing she would not was tough to rationalize.

"What's wrong? I don't know a lot about you, Hallie. Talk to me. Don't you live with your parents?" Amir asked, being so in tune with me that he knew something was out of rhythm.

I wanted to tell him it was such a long story that I did not want to go into it. It was painful. I did not want to relive or retell my history. I wanted to keep our evening upbeat, but he wanted more than just a surface conversation. When he rubbed my hand, it made me understand he was not going to judge me.

Peeling back a layer, I said, "I live with my dad. He's great and I love him. My mom ..."

"You don't have to tell me about it if you don't want to," he voiced, making sure I knew he was not trying to push harder than I could handle.

"I don't think you want to hear it," I uttered, as I sipped more of my delicious drink.

Not letting me off the hook, he said, "I'd love to know if you're up to telling me."

"She's a junkie. I don't know how or why, but drugs came before her family, and she left me and my dad. She comes in and out of our lives ... and really ... I don't know if she is okay or not. I feel a lot of my insecurity comes because my mom is missing from my life. I know that sounds stupid. I'm old enough to take ownership of my own problems."

"No, no, I know exactly what you're saying. My dad is there, but he's so focused on work that he couldn't care less about asking me what I want to do. My home life drives me crazy. Sometimes he looks at me like I have ruined his life by just being here. I don't understand it. I didn't do anything to deserve it. Sometimes I feel like I don't belong. I work extra hard to prove to him that I want to please him and nothing works. He hates me."

"I'm sure your dad doesn't hate you, Amir."

"You don't walk in my shoes, and you don't live in my house. Please don't tell me what I know to be true."

"I'm sorry," I said, sensing that he was becoming upset. "Okay, let's take the conversation off of parents. I saw Coach Strong talking to you in PE."

"Yeah, he wants me to try out for his football team," Amir shrugged.

Not understanding, I said, "They are already into the season."

"Yeah, you're right. He wants me to just come out and get to work," Amir replied.

Getting excited about the possibility, I tried to encourage him. "Really? Oh my gosh! That would be so great. I have seen you in PE, and you're like all over the place. You know you can jump high. What position does he want you to play? I don't think it's quarterback because I haven't seen you throw the ball. I'm sure you're not kicking because we've got a white boy for that. It's got to be wide receiver or DB because you're not big enough to be a lineman."

"What! What you know about football?" he smiled.

I am pretty sure he was impressed with my knowledge. "I told you, I'm a daddy's girl. He taught me all about the game. He probably wanted a son."

Amir laughed. "Yeah, the coach wants me to be a DB."

"So when are you going to practice? Oh my gosh, you can't go to practice because who's going to help me learn to flip?" I moaned.

"Hallie, quit tripping. You know how to flip. But you ain't got to worry. I'm not going out for no football team. Nah, that's for punks," Amir said seriously.

"Wait, okay, why is the football team for punks? You're tripping. That sounds like somebody's scared to put on the equipment and get out there," I said, calling him out.

I was really enjoying my conversation with Amir. We were going back and forth and just being able to talk to each other and have real-life conversation. I wasn't trying to be cute. I wasn't trying to be anybody but Hallie, and he was digging me. Because I felt comfortable, I went all the way there.

"You know, word's out that guys who work at gyms are a little on the funny side. You can squash all that if you get on the field," I said, believing that would make him want to give the game a try.

"Unlike you," Amir replied quickly, "I don't care what other people think of me. Being in a sport isn't going to make or break me. I'm going to school to get an education. I don't need to be a jock to feel important."

"Let's be clear, you're a junior and nobody even knows who you are. You're a hit at Cheertowne, but what good does that do you at Lockwood? You could help the team. We've struggled the last two games in the secondary. If you were out there, you could change it and turn it all around."

"I don't want to be on the football team, all right. Dang! Why you keep pressing me with that?" Amir banged on the table.

Not appreciating his demeanor, I blurted out, "Why you getting upset? I'm just telling you that at least you gotta try."

CHAPTER 4

Please Go

We're in a restaurant, Amir, and I'm not gonna get loud and crazy with you. I think it's stupid that you won't get out there on the football team and try to play," I yelled. I could not hold my big mouth. I tried and failed.

Amir flinched and said, "Whatever, woman, you don't even know what you want. What's stupid is you want status and are afraid to let your heart really like somebody for who they are on the inside. If they are not a baller, and your friends don't know him, you gonna turn your back."

"What? Are you calling me shallow?" I huffed. I crossed my arms in defiance.

"I call it like I see it, baby," Amir said. He wasn't trying to smooth over what he was insinuating.

"What about jerk? That's your name," I said. I stood up and grabbed some water that was on our table and doused his face. I was burning up. "I do like you. But I push the people I care about. Gosh!"

I could not get out of that restaurant fast enough. The only problem was when I got outside, I realized I did not drive. My car was at the gym. So I reached into my purse to call Charli to see if she could come and sweep me up. But before I could get my phone—in the blink of an eye—my purse was snatched from me. I tried to scream, but a strong hand covered my mouth. Amir spun me around like a top and then his lips were touching mine. We had just been so hot and angry with each other, and now we had heat and passion going in a different way.

However, I did not know what I was doing. Not only was I caught off guard, but his tongue was rolling around in my mouth. I did not know which way my tongue should roll, and it kept getting caught up. I was so awkward. It was like

I was thinking too hard about it all, and I did not know how to let my body just relax and enjoy the moment. I had no experience in this area.

I was not a virgin, but I had never kissed a guy. Last year I got busy with this senior dude, but there was no intimacy. There was no real connection. The guy was just trying to feel good, and I was trying to dull my life's pain. He did not care about connecting with me, and now that Amir was trying to do that, I was a mess.

Amir's mouth opened a little bit, and he placed his hands on both sides of my head. I could feel that he cared. I could feel that he wanted to be with me. I could feel that this was right, but as I tried to express myself back that same way, I bit him.

"I'm so sorry. Oh my gosh. Did that hurt?" I said when I saw a little blood.

He just said ouch and started laughing. I could not believe he was snickering. This was serious to me. I really wanted to know how to do this, but he thought it was funny that I did not know. Call me sensitive, but at that moment I was appalled.

"How could you laugh?"

"I'm not laughing at you. I'm laughing at the moment. Ease up. Can't you tell by the kiss that I care? Don't give me a hard time about this. We've always been able to talk, Hallie," Amir said, trying touch me.

"Yeah, we've been able to talk but not laugh at each other." I walked away. But where could I go? I was stranded without my car, so I turned back to Amir. "Can you just take me home, please?"

"Can I talk to you?" he said. He walked over and grabbed my hand.

When I turned to face to him my cheeks were covered with salty tears. It looked like I was the one who just had H_2O splashed in my face or something.

"What is wrong? Talk to me."

"No, just take me home, please. Take me back to get my car or something. Let's just get out of here," I struggled to say. I was really embarrassed because we were starting to look like some kind of reality show.

Amir flared his nose and got a little salty. "See, that's what I'm saying, you care too much about what other people think."

"I know I'm not perfect. Is that what you want me to say? Can you just take me back to get my car? Please, Amir?" I cried.

"It was just a kiss. You'll get it. It's no big deal. Come here, we can try it again," Amir said, as he put his arm around my waist and pulled me to him.

I pushed him hard. Finally he listened and we got in his car. We did not say anything all the way to the gym. When we arrived, I quickly got out and headed to my car. Amir followed me.

"Just leave me alone, Amir. I'm sorry. I guess I wasn't ready for all of this. I wasn't trying to mislead you or anything like that, I just ..."

He pulled me to him and held me really tight. At that point I didn't have to keep explaining myself. I didn't have to keep making excuses. I didn't have to say I was sorry. He was there, and his actions showed me he cared.

"I wish I had a mom to teach me all this stuff," I blurted out. It was hard to hold in my deepest feelings. "If she was in my life, and if she was with me, she would be my mom instead of out in the streets doing who knows what. If she was around, I'd know how to do simple stuff like ... kiss."

Being really sweet and understanding, Amir said, "Don't take this the wrong way, but I couldn't imagine your mom teaching you how to French kiss. Ease up, you're stressing. I'm here. Heck, for all I know I could've been doing it wrong. I don't want you to get all wound up."

"I just wish my mom was here. She and I could at least talk about me getting nervous when a boy puts his lips on mine. Oh my gosh. I can't believe I'm even saying this to you."

He turned my face to his and said, "Hallie, do you like me?"

Without thinking, I said, "A lot."

"Then let's go for this again."

He kissed my left cheek, and then he kissed my right cheek. He cupped my face with his hands once again. He kissed my forehead, and before I knew it he was kissing my lips, once, twice, then three times. Naturally, my lips part- ed, and we were kissing, tonguing, and enjoying each other. I knew he had stepped back from me because I could feel the breeze between us. How- ever, my eyes were still closed, and my lips were still puckered. He didn't dare laugh. I guess he was staring like a guy who was smitten.

When I opened my eyes he said, "That's all for now. When you let what we're feeling take over, you don't have to get caught up in whether you're doing it right or wrong. I just need to know you like me. I just need to know you care. I just need to know you wanna try, and we'll figure out the rest."

"All right," I smiled, feeling good.

Did this mean that he was my boyfriend? I couldn't ask, but I knew I did not want anyone else to touch me. I thought it was going to be impossible for me to learn how to flip, but Amir helped me to overcome that phobia. I never thought I'd have a guy who stuck around and was there for me after what happened last year.

I didn't want to leave his side, but he said, "Go on home. I'll call you later. I need to talk to my boss inside."

I wanted to feel his lips against mine one more time before I left, but the memory would have to do for now. When he got to the door, Lexus let him in. She looked over at me with a brutal stare. She must have seen us connect. She was not happy but I surely was. Who needs a football player when you've got a gentleman?

"Hallie, seriously, girl, you are not performing it right. You're all over the place. Everyone
knows the routine except for you," Charli said to
me as delicately as she possibly could.

This was hard. I had practiced the routine
at home. I had it down. I had gone over my
moves again and again, but when it came time
to practice, they rearranged things. While that
may not have seemed like a big deal for most of
the squad, it threw the whole thing off for me.

I looked back over at the girls and most
of them were not happy with me. Arms were
folded. Eyes were rolling in my direction. It was
clear that I was the weak link they wanted to
cut out. Our first competition was coming up in
three weeks. I wanted to make excuses. I wanted
to tell Charli it wasn't my fault, and that she
should stop changing stuff. But if everyone else
got it except me, then it meant that I needed a
little more work.

Charli scolded, "Last couple of days we've
been staying after school, and you are nowhere
around. What's going on with you, Hallie? Is
there something more going on with your dad?
Are you having to work a job or something?"

"Why is she still on the team anyway?" the co-captain, Whitney, whined so loudly that even people in the parking lot could hear her.

I knew our squad was more than just a cheering team for the boys. We had a mission. We were trying to win a state cheerleading title and hopefully qualify to compete nationally at the ESPN cheerleading competition in Orlando. There was a lot riding on us, and I didn't want to let anyone down.

However, it was not like I wasn't trying. Actually, I was getting really tired of putting up with the backstabbing talk. Hearing negative talk did not affect some folks, but it crushed me. My team needed to know that I was not okay with it.

I rushed over to Whitney and said, "What? If you have something to say to me … if you want to talk about me … then I'm right here. You don't have to do it behind my back. What do you wanna say?" I pushed her. "What, cat's got your tongue? You're too scared to say anything now? I'm standing right here. You wanna talk about me? You wanna bring it on? You think I can't cut it? Tell me now, witch!"

Whitney ran behind Charli. "Can you please get your friend? She's crazy and I don't fight."

Randal gave me a look that said, *Whoa, settle down!* Eva and Ella pulled me to the side. I could tell they both wanted to strangle me.

"What are you doing?" Ella exclaimed.

In a more direct tone, Eva added, "You can't go around pushing on folks. You're gonna get thrown off the team. Is that what you want?"

"You two think I don't deserve to be here either. So what difference does it make if I get kicked off or if I quit?"

"Ain't no need in having an attitude with us," Eva said. "Charli's right. We're here after school the last couple of weeks going over these routines. You have been MIA. I know it wasn't mandatory, but everybody thinks that you're the first person who needs to be here to practice. So what's up? Charli might buy that bull about your lack of cash flow, but please, we know your dad's got it going on right now with his car repair shop. Ain't nobody buying new cars. Everybody's getting what they got fixed. Your dad's raking in the dough. So where you been?"

If I could've socked my friend, I would have. They thought I was goofing off when I was working overtime on my tumbling. But I was already way too heated, so I just balled my fist and walked away.

Coach Woods stepped outside of her office and yelled, "Hallie, let me see you right now, please."

I didn't actually realize I was being so forceful with Whitney. However, I was not going to try to justify why I was all in her face. She was talking about me, and she did deserve a little shove so she would shut up. Just because she deserved it, however, didn't make it right. If Coach wanted me off the team, fine. Maybe if the girls knew I was working out at Cheertowne, they would cut me some slack and not be so hard on me, but it wasn't any of their business. My girls especially should know I wasn't slacking off. For them to think all of this didn't matter to me pissed me off. Cheering was my life. I was trying to do everything in my power to get better.

"Yes?" I said, as I stepped into Coach Woods's office with an attitude that was truly disrespectful.

"Okay, you need to step out of my office and come right back in. You are *not* going to talk to me like I'm one of your peers. Let's try this again."

"Yes, ma'am," I said humbly.

I stepped outside of her door, knocked, and waited for her to respond.

She said, "Come in."

I answered, "Yes, ma'am, you wanted to see me?"

"Much better," Coach said. "Listen, Hallie, sit down and let's talk."

I could tell what she had to say to me was not gonna be fun for her to verbalize or fun for me to listen to. We all had a running joke about when Coach Woods called you into her office and asked you to have a seat that it meant you were in severe trouble. She was breathing deeply like it was affecting her. I could tell she did not want to give me this bad news.

Seeing her struggle, I teared up. She came from around her desk when she saw my face. Coach placed her hand on my hand and then grabbed it hard.

She said, "I know you want to be on this team, but I need you to help me keep you on this team.

You have potential and more than that, you have heart. I *wanted* you to be here, and there were some things you told me that you were going to work on. However, we're a game into the season, and all the cheerleaders are jumping high. Your jumps don't compare. I need to shuffle things around because you clearly need to be in the back on some of these formations. You don't have some of the skills that you truly need," she sighed. "You get thrown off and you can't adjust. Then at the football game, you were struggling too. When it's halftime and the girls are flipping, I understand you're not there with the tumbling, but you cannot run off the football field. That is unacceptable. I really need an explanation, Hallie. What is going on with you?"

"I don't know, Coach. I just feel like I'm breaking. I look at everybody, and they're such polished cheerleaders that mentally I don't think I can compete. I haven't been slacking off. I didn't want to tell any of them because I don't want anyone to have any expectations that I can't meet, but I've been going to Cheertowne and working on my tumbling skills. I've almost got it."

She made cheer fingers in the air and blurted, "Well, that's exciting. I need to know this stuff."

"But what if I can't do it? What if I spend a month learning how to tumble and I come back with nothing? I'd really be the laughing stock then, Coach. Please don't tell anybody," I pleaded.

"I won't," Coach Woods said. She took a deep breath and then delivered more tough news. "But Hallie, you gotta give me one hundred percent. We compete soon. If you don't have the tumbling, if those jumps aren't higher, and if you can't get the routine down, I will have no choice but take you off the squad."

I wiped my eyes and nodded. I did not want any more special favors. She had already done that by putting me on the team in the first place. I knew it was up to me to do what I needed to do and be all that she needed me to be. I was going to do that.

"All right, go get yourself together and keep working on you. You can get this. Don't make me have to pull the plug, okay?

"Yes, ma'am."

She gave me a big hug. That was supposed to make me feel better. I felt worse.

"Hallie, girl, come give Uncle Joe some love. Dang, you grown up on me, curving out and everything," my mom's brother said. He reeked of alcohol.

He was hugging me inappropriately, real tight. It reminded me of when I was seven. He was baby-sitting me, and he was preparing my bath. I was waiting for him to leave so I could get in the tub, but he told me he saw nude women all the time and went and got a bunch of magazines. Uncle Joe told me when I got older that I would look like that. Of course I told my parents because I didn't think anything was wrong with it, and my dad knocked out one of his teeth. When my parents had their split, my dad forbid me to visit my mom's side of the family. But I knew if I was going to have a chance of finding her, I needed to talk to her relatives. They might know where she was. So I'd gone to Watts Road.

When I took my hands and pushed him in his chest real hard, he shouted, "Dang, you got muscles and stuff."

Stepping farther back, I uttered, "Just tell me where she is, Uncle, come on."

"My sister didn't even recognize me the last time I saw her. She came over here last week asking for some money. I don't think you wanna see her, Hallie," he said, being the protective uncle he should be.

"Please, just tell me where she is," I begged.

"I don't even know if it's safe for you to go over there. I can't go with you right now. I got a few tricks coming by the house for a celebration with a couple of my partners. I can go over there with you tomorrow."

"Just please tell me where it is," I insisted.

"She's staying at Big Daddy Wayne's house. It's the crack place two streets over. Tell them who you're looking for, for goodness' sake, or they won't even let you up in there. You look too clean and too broke at the same time. Your young behind ... be safe, young blood. You ain't letting no nappy-head boy pop it, are you?" Uncle Joe asked, looking me up and down like I was a pin-up model. "I don't wanna have to whoop up on somebody. Why we gotta be kin?" he muttered.

"Gross," I thought. "Bye. Thanks." I bolted to the car.

It definitely was not the best neighborhood. Folks strung out everywhere. People feeling each other up in public. Gunfire going off. I could not believe my mom really wanted to live like this and be so high that she did not even know her own name. There were zombies walking around in the street. They were so messed up that they thought my car was an alien ship.

My mom had taught me one lesson, and that was to not ever touch a pipe. Shucks, I didn't even want a cigarette. I didn't want to get hooked because the last thing I wanted was to be pulled away from my family, my dreams, and myself. I wanted her to get help. I wanted her to know I still loved her. She needed to hear that I needed her. I needed to find her. There were no cars in front of Big Daddy Wayne's house, but I definitely knew which one it was, not only because it was in the exact spot that my uncle told me it would be in, but because there were several junkies standing all around the tore-up house begging for more crack or whatever it was they were trying to smoke.

"Home skillet, you got some money?" this one smelly, toothless, and bow-legged man asked.

Then I thought about my uncle. He thought I looked like I was broke? I must not look too broke because these folks tryna hit me up for cash.

"I'm here to see Alisha. Do you know Alisha?" I asked, showing her picture.

"I know Alisha. I'll tell you where she is if you got some money. Ten dollars," this lady bargained.

"Ma'am, I don't have ten dollars," I said to the lady whose breasts were hanging out for all the world to see.

She continued, "Five dollars."

"I don't have five dollars."

"You got anything? You must don't wanna know where Alisha is then."

"Alisha? Who said my name?" my mom suddenly appeared from behind the house.

I rushed over to her and grabbed the substance in her hand and threw it on the ground. She was trying to wrestle me, and people were fighting each other to get whatever I'd thrown out. It was mayhem, like twenty players on a football field scrambling to get a fumble.

"Mom, it's me. It's Hallie," I yelled, hoping that she would stop slapping me.

"Baby girl, that's you?" she said, coming out of her trance.

"Yes, Mom. It's me."

"Who is me? Oh, she look too good," this one slick man said.

He grabbed my mom and thrust his hand up her skirt. I was horrified.

She turned around and said, "Boom Dog, not now! My baby girl came. Just not now."

Boom Dog said, "That's *your* daughter? Dang, I didn't know you could produce them like this. Wassup, Ms. Thang?"

"Get on back, mister," I said, wishing I was anywhere but here.

"Boom Dog? Big Daddy Wayne? Where the heck was I?" I thought. Then I screamed, "Mom, you need to come with me. We need to go!"

She put her hands between us. "Go where? I'm home, honey."

"And if you wanna help Mom pay the rent, why don't you come home with me," the nasty Boom Dog said and grabbed my shirt.

"Get off of me," I said, wishing I had a knife.

"Not my baby, okay?" my mom defended.

"What? All I need to do is get with her and I'll clear you. I can put you in a room. I can talk to Big Daddy Wayne, and you'll be straight. Let her pay your rent. Matter a fact, I'm sure he'd wanna get a piece of her too."

At that moment all I could think of was that whatever I was gonna have to do in my life, I wanted to earn an honest living. I would rather work at a fast food restaurant, mop the floors, cut grass, or anything that was hard labor before having no job and having to sell myself or my child to be able to eat or have a roof over my head. I wasn't even aware of what was happening, but the guy called Boom Dog called over two other guys and they picked me up. They carried me to the backyard and started tugging at my clothes.

Mom came around yelling and screaming with some of her other junkie friends. "Get off my child," she screeched.

I knew why my dad didn't want me to find her. He didn't want me to be a part of this. He didn't want me in harm's way. However, I had been determined to find her because I cared for her. I was doing it because I thought I could show her a better way. I was doing it because I thought she loved me enough to leave all of this behind. But she was in too deep. She couldn't help herself much less help me. She started pulling off her clothes right in front of me. She told a couple of ladies I didn't know to do the same.

When the strong, thuggish men were distracted by all of the nudity, they let me go. My mom screamed out, "Run, Hallie, and don't come back here, baby. Go! I don't want you to see Mommy like this. I'm sorry, baby."

I wanted to go back and hug her, but the sight I saw made me vomit, and I hadn't even eaten all day. Why did drugs have to mess up my mom's life?

When Boom Dog started coming back toward me, my mom cried out, "Hallie? Go! Just please go!"

CHAPTER 5

Highly Upset

My life was spiraling out of control because I had just seen my naked mother offering her pathetically wasted body to some lowlife to save me from a terrible fate. That image would forever be seared in my memory, but I wanted to erase it completely from my brain. There was no way that I would ever be able do that. She looked dirty. She was skinny. She smelled. Her teeth were crumbling. She looked trashy, and she was selling her body to get a fix. It was too much. The only thing I knew to do was get drunk and hopefully forget it all. With shaky hands I dialed my girl Randal.

"Where you guys going?" I asked bluntly.

"Um, hello to you too," Randal replied. "Eva said that senior running back Waxton is having a party. Come swing by his place. We're on our way there."

"I *called* you!" Ella yelled out in the background.

"Me too!" Charli said.

"And don't come dressed like a nun," Eva added.

I did not even care what I had on. I was not going home because my dad would be able to tell I was upset. Plus now that I knew my pops had a girlfriend, the last thing I wanted to do was go home unannounced. I told him I would be hanging out for the evening, and that was exactly what I was going to do. Once I got the directions, I headed over to Waxton's house.

The team was relaxing because it was a bye week, which meant we did not have a game. I hoped that the bye week would not halt our momentum because our team needed to tighten up on defense. Their secondary looked weak. If the opposing team was throwing long bombs left and right, we could not deflect them or intercept them. We needed new players or at least one.

Amir had talent, but I was not even going to stress with the fact that he did not want to play. One thing I realized was people had to live their own lives. However, if I was taking his advice about tumbling and receiving his help to become a better gymnast, the least he could do was take my advice as well and play football.

When I got there, I did not see my girls. Obviously, I had beaten them. They were probably in some nearby restaurant bathroom primping. I did not know what Waxton's parents did or where they were, but they had an open bar downstairs. I walked right up to it and told a guy, who I recognized from school, to give me something strong.

"Can I see your ID?" Pinecone had the nerve to ask me.

I said with attitude, "Are you serious, Pinecone? Who in here *is* the right age?"

Pinecone threw up his hands. "Dang! Chill, lil' mama. I was just playing. Ease out, ease out! Here you go. You need something quick to take the edge off. What you do? Catch your man cheating?"

"Nah, I caught my mom selling herself to her pimp for drugs," I barked. I tossed back my drink.

"Oh, dang. TMI, girlfriend. Too much information. For real, for real." Pinecone frowned.

I looked at the empty little glass. "Two more, please. And next time don't ask me questions if you don't want to know the answer."

He filled up that little glass and gave me another one. "You need two shots. Cut your mama some slack. That diamond around your neck cost money and had to be paid for."

I touched my necklace, and I thought about a happier time in my life when all was right in the world. I had just turned thirteen. The lovely solitaire was the gift my parents gave me. Why did things have to go all wild? Why did my mom have to lose her job? Why did my parents fall out of love with each other? Why, why, why? So many questions ... no freaking answers.

I lost track of how many shots I took, but I was feeling good. When Ella and Randal found me, I was out of it. Luckily, I could tell it was them.

"Hey girls!" I slurred and promptly fell down.

Ella caught me and said, "What is going on with you? Oh my gosh, your breath stinks!

How many of these did you give her?" she asked Pinecone. He had a guilty look, but he was not saying nothing.

Ella asked him again. Pinecone shrugged. She looked at me for an answer, but I laughed and shrugged. It was a happy world. I was so mellow.

Randal said, "Hallie, why are you drinking like this? You're a mess."

"If you're going to be so high socially ... I mean high senility ... I mean high—"

Randal interrupted, "High society."

Hugging her, I said, "Yeah, you knew what I was trying to say. Then get out of my face! Go, go ..."

At that moment, I saw Amir or a guy that looked like him talking to Lexus from Cheer-towne. Amir was frowning. I bobbled my way over to them and cut into their conversation.

"You, you ... like him don't you?" I said to her. "But he likes me ..."

"Hallie, you been drinking," Amir said, clearly bummed out by my behavior.

"Give this man a million dollars! You are correct, sir," I said to him.

Lexus said to him, "Ugh, and *this* is what you want? What does she have that I don't have?"

"Nothing, I have nothing that you don't have. I have no mother. I have no mother. Did I say I have no mother?" And I fell toward Amir.

Ella and Randal came up to him and Ella said, "Could you help us get our friend home?"

"Amir, you just gonna leave? We're talking," Lexus said.

I mouthed "Sorrrrry," and then he said something to her and we headed outside. I passed by somebody who had a bottle. I grabbed it and chugged some more. When Amir saw me, he took it and threw the bottle away.

"What are you doing?" he growled. "Why are you doing this to yourself? You're too good to make stupid choices."

"I'm too stupid to make stupid choices says the man with all the baller potential who doesn't want to get hit. You scared of getting hit, little baby?" I teased.

I must have upset him because he backed away. Randal and Ella came up on both sides of me. "We got her," Ella said. "Can you just follow us to her car?"

"I also have my own car here," he said.

Ella rationalized, "Well, could you take her home, and we'll follow you in her car? Then you could bring us back."

Amir nodded and Randal asked me, "Where are your keys, Hallie?"

"Keys, what are keys?" I said to them.

"Hallie, where are your *car* keys!" Ella demanded. She slapped my face lightly.

Thinking I was sobering up, I overreacted and yelled, "Don't hit my face! You remember my dad slapped me, and I didn't like it then, so don't slap my face now, okay? Just. Don't."

Ella whispered, "Hallie, quit tripping! This guy likes you, and you are being so stupid."

"I don't feel good," I said.

Amir said, "Well, you need to throw up right now because I don't want any of that in my car. Talk about dads … mine would have a fit. Throw up right now."

"Don't be so hard on her," Ella said to Amir.

Randal turned to Ella. "Let him handle her. He obviously cares."

"Yeah, but he doesn't need to be so rough," Ella fretted.

Randal replied, "Whatever, you're the one who just slapped her."

Ella said, "I was just trying to get her to wake up, and it wasn't that hard."

I said, "I hear you guys talking and …"

The next thing I knew, a whole bunch of stuff inside of me came out all over my girls' feet. I could not even apologize because I felt so weak. My head was spinning like a top. I was done.

"We're going to wash off. You take her home. She lives right by the school."

"Let me see her license," he requested.

They went into my purse. Ella handed him my license. He plugged it into his GPS. He made sure I was fastened in, and then the two of us were off. I still felt wobbly. Every move he made felt like I was in a bumper car.

"Could you slow down?" I huffed.

"Could you not be drunk?" he fumed.

"Why would you do this, Hallie? Why you get drunk like this? I don't even know why I'm talking to you. You're not even fully conscious right now."

"Not even fully conscious right now…" I mimicked back at him.

Amir was upset with me, and I was upset with myself. But what was done was done. I wanted to feel better, but unfortunately I felt worse.

"Amir, you naughty boy, get your hands out of my shirt," I teased, completely intoxicated as Amir helped me out of his car.

I am sure that he was the perfect gentleman, but it felt fun to play with him.

He corrected, "Hallie, my hand is on your arm. Come on. I just want to confirm this is your house. This is what was on your driver's license, but I don't want to bring you to the wrong door. Is your dad going to be cool with me bringing you home?"

"Oh, you got to kiss me. I want to get my dad back. I remember I came home and saw him with this lady. We could do the same thing. Come on, come on. Kiss me!" I said, as I puckered my lips and weaved in and out on my wobbly legs.

I was trying to jump on Amir, but my balance was way off, and I completely missed his body. When I fell to the ground, he bent down to pull me up, and I yanked him down on top of me.

"The ground's all wet! Come on, Hallie, I don't want to take you in your house all dirty. Hallie, stop playing," Amir said in an irritated tone.

"You don't want to kiss me? You want to pick up where we left off? I know how to kiss now. I'm not going to bite your lip. What if you bite mine?" I thought that I had my flirt on.

"Get up!" he said harshly.

Suddenly, I heard a boom. Amir looked up and started panicking. It was then that I figured my daddy had come out and slammed the door shut behind him.

My father rushed over to the two of us. "What is going on over here? Why is my daughter's shirt practically open? And she's *drunk*? Young man, who are you? I don't believe this!" my dad said coldly, as he took me by the arm and pushed Amir back.

"No, no, no, sir," Amir said, putting his arms in the air. "You've got the wrong idea."

"The wrong idea," my father yelled. "You bring my daughter home drunk, her clothes aren't even put together, and you're telling me I can't make out what I see."

"Calm down, sir. Please, let me explain," Amir said as calmly as he could. Lights started to pop on in the houses around the neighborhood.

My dad was beyond pissed off. "Calm down? This is my child! Don't tell me to calm down!"

"Dad, why all the fussing? It's a sun-shiny day. Wait, where's the sun?" I said to the big full moon.

"Hallie, go inside the house," my dad screamed at me.

"Aye, aye, captain," I said with a salute.

Amir continued pleading his case, "Sir, I'm not trying to offend you or be disrespectful. I was just trying to explain."

"Get off my property. Where's my daughter's car?" my father ranted.

"Why are you yelling, Dad? You should have some of the shots I had. I'm so happy. I'm forgetting all about how I saw Mom at the crack house," I blurted. Oops. I quickly put my hand over my mouth and laughed, knowing that I'd told my dad something I should have kept to myself.

"You *what*? Where have you been, Hallie? And where's your car? Please tell me you weren't drinking and driving."

Ella and Randal pulled up at that moment. I pointed to my ride. I was smiling again because in my intoxicated brain, all was right with the world.

I whispered, "Dad, I like him. No fussing at the guy." Then I started crying. "Dad, if you hit him like you hit me, he'll never come back."

"Hallie, get yourself together, girl!" my father beseeched.

Ella could tell there was drama, so she cut in, "Mr. Ray, let us explain. This is not Amir's fault. We asked him to bring Hallie home."

"Why is she drunk?" my father demanded.

"When we got to the party, she was already trashed," Ella confessed, sending me a contrite look.

Again I smiled. At that moment I really had no clue she was getting me deeper in trouble. But Randal did, and she hit Ella in the arm.

Realizing she wasn't helping the situation, Ella said, "Sir, I mean, she had something to drink. We got her out of there immediately. We knew that since we needed to get her car home, we could ask Amir to help. He is a guy from our junior class, and he is a responsible driver—"

"How do you know he's a responsible driver? You ever seen him drive before?" my father grilled her.

Ella pitifully tried explaining, "Well, it's just that—"

My dad cut her off and said, "Okay, save it."

Amir was frustrated too. "Sir, I got your daughter home in one piece. I promise you, I had nothing to do with her drinking. I don't support it. I told her it was wrong."

"Still doesn't explain her clothes practically off her body. Just go." My dad pointed toward the street and off our lot.

"No, Amir, don't go," I begged.

"Hallie, what are you doing?" my dad asked. "Ella, Randal, y'all get her in the house right now."

My girls pulled me away. My father said more harsh words to Amir. Amir turned back around, stood there, and took it. My girls led me to the door.

Randal said, "He was supposed to take us back to the party, but now ..."

"Just get her inside," Ella said. "We'll have to call Charli. She'll swing through and pick us up."

Limp as a cooked piece of spaghetti, I said, "I'm sorry, y'all. I'm so sorry. Y'all love me, don't you? Kisses, kisses ..."

"Hallie, you know you're going to be grounded forever," Ella said to me with a quick shake of her head.

"And if you throw up on our feet again ...," Randal threatened. "You're dad won't have to kill you, because I will."

Ella said, "Right, that was gross, Hallie."

"I threw up on your feet? Oh y'all, I'm sorry," I said breathlessly.

Randal said she was going to the kitchen to get me a glass of water. Water was probably a good idea because I felt my heart start racing.

I squealed, "Ella, you got to get my dad. I think I'm going to die. My chest, it hurts really bad!"

Ella shouted, "Randal hurry up with the water! This happened to Eva a couple of times. When you drink too much alcohol too fast sometimes it does weird things. That's why you need to lay off the bottle, girl. You know you can't handle anything, much less two or three or four shots of who knows what Pinecone had you drinking."

"I know, right? That bartender liked me. Do you think Amir hates me?" I asked with fingers crossed.

"Girl, he is so cute, but you took that boy through a whole bunch of drama. I don't know if he's ever going to talk to you again," Ella laughed.

I just looked at her dumbfounded. Randal could not get the water in my mouth fast enough. I chugged it and it did seem to soothe my heart. Randal went back to the bathroom and got washcloths. She brought a wet cloth to my face and wiped it really hard.

I complained. "Ouch!"

Randal said, "Hold still, we're not putting you in the shower, but we need to clean you up a little bit."

I was in and out of it, but I could tell they were talking about me. Ella mentioned something about that this was all because of my mom. Randal said she could only imagine how I must feel. Seeing my mom messing up her life that way, I knew they understood why I had to drink my troubles away.

Waving my hand in front of them, I said, "I'm okay. I'm here. I hear y'all."

"Yeah, okay," Ella said, pacifying me. She knew I still wasn't fully myself. "Let's get in bed now. Come on. Get under the covers."

My dad came to my bedroom door and said, "Ladies, thank you for being really good friends to Hallie."

Ella said, "No problem, sir. We just wanted you to know that we did tell Amir to bring her home. It's our fault. Don't be mad at him."

My dad responded, "It's fine. It's over. I'm glad she's safe. Do I need to take you guys somewhere?"

Ella said, "No, thank you. Charli should be picking us up any minute. We texted her a while ago."

"Okay, thanks. Hallie's got a lot she's dealing with, but she's blessed to have good friends like y'all. If I need to talk to your parents to let them know where you are, I can do that."

"No, sir. We did that too."

"This is just great. So now they know my daughter got drunk," my dad said. "They're really not going to like you hanging out with her now. I don't know why Hallie didn't think about the consequences."

"Sir, you know my mom doesn't judge like that," Ella said reflecting on how down Mama B always was.

Then Randal spoke up, "And my parents love Hallie. Don't worry, they will get on her for making a bad choice, but they won't keep me from hanging out with her."

"I appreciate that, girls. I just want my daughter to know I love her. Just because some bad things have happened to her doesn't mean she has to bring more bad things upon herself. I'm truly disappointed," my father sighed.

There was a horn honking. They all left my room, and I wiped tears from my face. I guess lying there in the quiet by myself made me able to rationalize better. I had made a dumb choice and completely embarrassed myself. Worse than that, I had gotten Amir, the guy I really liked, in trouble with my father. I had also made my father upset. I knew no temporary buzz was worth the humiliating lesson learned.

My final humiliation was the most excruciating headache the next morning. It felt like someone had taken my head and knocked it against the pavement. I actually put my hands on my head to make sure I had not cracked my skull. In addition to thinking I had a head injury, my body felt as if it had been hit by a truck. I felt worse than awful and less than zero.

I rolled over and looked at the clock and saw that it was two in the afternoon. I jumped up immediately and wondered if I had forgotten cheerleading practice or school or church, but then I realized it was Saturday. My dad was kind enough to let me chill. However, it was time for me to get up.

Then it dawned on me. My dad was probably so ticked. I thought really hard on everything that transpired the night before. Reliving it all broke my heart. I still could not get over the fact that my mom sold her body for drugs. And she had to give her body over yesterday so the thugs would not break me. As mad as I was at her for living in such a horrible way, I wanted to hug her and thank her for protecting me in the end.

Then I remembered my bout with the alcohol. Pinecone must have known better, but at least now I knew that I never needed to drink to excess again. But how did I get home? Then I smiled, remembering Amir Knight.

I knew he had to think horribly of me, but I knew he was certainly the one who came to my rescue. And then my girls Ella and Randal having my back and making sure I got home safely. I did not deserve their friendship, but I was going to make certain I let them know I was appreciative.

"Oh, so I see somebody's up, huh? Well, we need to talk right now. Drinking, Hallie, seriously?" my dad said. He could see that I was hurting as he came into my room and saw me sitting up in my bed with my knees close to my chest.

I humbly said, "I'm sorry, Dad. I owe you such a huge apology. Sorry."

Needing answers, my dad said, "And this young man ... he explained to me that he wasn't trying to take advantage of you. That he didn't give you any alcohol."

"No, Dad."

"Well, who is he?"

"He's this guy I've been talking to. At Cheer-towne, he's my instructor, but he goes to my school. I'm almost close to flipping and realizing my dreams because of him. He's a really, really nice guy."

"Knowing all the facts, I know he cares. I feel bad that I was real rude to the young brother," my dad admitted.

"You hate me, huh?" I said to my dad as I hung my head in shame.

"I'm disappointed. You know I don't allow you to go looking for your mom, particularly not by yourself, Hallie. I know you want to see her and make sure she's okay and all, but dang, girl. No telling what could have happened to you down there. What would have happened if you didn't make it back here? I don't know what I would have done. I just wish you would think. We're going to fix all of this. We're going to have a nice family dinner to discuss it. You and me."

I leapt out of bed and went to hug his neck. "Daddy-daughter time?" I asked

"Don't try to be all nice and sweet. You are going to be grounded, but I do want to have a chance to talk with this young man, and I need you to do me a favor too."

"Anything, Dad. I certainly owe you for not being blazing mad. I just needed to not feel the pain, ya know?"

"No, there is *never* an excuse to drink. You

don't know, someone could have put something in that drink. We have a lot to talk about. You do owe me," he repeated.

"Okay, name it. What do you want me to do? Straighten out your closet, come to the shop and clean up down there? Get your files organized? What? Name it, Dad and it's done," I said.

"I'd like to have dinner this week with Amir."

"Wow, that's great," I said, thinking that was not bad at all.

"Good, let's call him now, and I'd like for Greta to be there as well," he said, ushering in the bad news.

"Huh? That lady?"

"She's not just some lady, Hallie. We have to find a way to move on with our lives. I want you to be respectful and get to know her. Can you do that for me?"

A couple of days later, I still did not have the answer to my father's question as I sat beside Amir at the dinner table. However, I had to look at this lady make goo-goo eyes at my dad. None of us were saying anything. It was really an uncomfortable moment. I could see in her eyes she wanted to tell me she would be the perfect step-monster, but hopefully she could get from my body language that I did not want her any-where around. Amir was trying to tell to me to cool down, ease up, not be so hard, but he didn't dare say anything because he knew I was broken.

"So, young man, tell me about yourself."

"Well, sir, I—"

Before he could say anything, there was a hard knock on the door. The harsh sound startled us all. I shrugged.

"Hallie, you're not expecting anybody are you?" my dad said to me.

And I looked back at him like, *No. Are you expecting anybody?* Plus that somebody was going to almost beat the door down. My father got up and went to the door, and all of a sudden Mom pushed him back and rushed into the din-ing room.

My mother frantically bellowed, "Where's my baby? I need to see her. I need to tell her I'm so sorry. I need to make sure she's okay. Oh my gosh ..."

"Mom?" I said, still hating that she looked tore up from the floor up.

"Mom, I'm okay," I was slightly embarrassed that my new guy friend was there to see how fragile and unkempt my mom was, but I didn't want her to leave. I needed to see if she was ready to leave that crazy world, but my dad grabbed her arm.

He barked, "What are you doing coming over to my house? And how'd you get here? Who's with you? I don't want anyone knowing where we live, thinking they can rob us to pay for your habits. And what was going on with my daughter a few days ago? What are you talking about, her safety? Hallie, we need to talk about all that you saw. Get out, Alisha! Get out!" my dad practically demanded.

My mom said, "I don't want to leave right now. I want to talk to my baby. You can't make me leave!"

"Oh, yes, I can. Remember I have a court order keeping you off the premises."

"A court order, Dad?" I was shocked. "She's my mom. You can't keep her away from me."

"Yes, I can! I don't tell you all the things that go on with your mom. She steals from this house."

"I'm sorry, baby," my mama said. "I'm sorry. Please just let me talk to you, Hallie. I don't want you—"

"Get out of my house, right now!" my father roared louder than a real lion.

"I need help. You got to understand. I need help," my mother cried.

"Well, go get help then. You're not getting any more from here. You've burned your last bridge," my dad said. With a huge shove, he pushed my mom out of the house. She fell to the ground, and he slammed the door shut.

I wanted to get him to move so I could go outside. However, he stood firmly in front of the door almost daring me to open it. It was a very charged moment, and we were highly upset.

CHAPTER 6
Do It

Dad, just get outta my way!" I yelled at the top of my lungs, as my eyes filled with tears.

I physically tried to move my father. However, he would not budge. My dad was angry, but I was angrier.

"You're not going anywhere. Sit down. Let's finish our dinner, and let's pretend like she never even came here," he tried selling me, like the time he told me spinach tasted like cake so I would eat it.

I wanted to yell, "What kind of crack are you smoking? Mom is the one high, but you're making absolutely no sense." Of course I wanted to keep all of my teeth, so I did not say anything.

My eyes turned red. Instinctively, I looked back at Amir who was glazed over by the whole ordeal, and I gave him a look signifying that I needed his help. I guess that was all he needed because he came straight over to the man of the house and pleaded my case.

The guy who had my heart and had forgiven me for my drunken scene days earlier said, "Sir, please just … just let me take her out. I will help her look for her mom. I'll bring her back. I won't let her go anywhere alone, sir."

When my dad looked away, I added, "Dad, if my mom leaves here and overdoses or something, I will never forgive you."

"Honey, just let her go," Greta came over to my father and said. It made my skin crawl that his girlfriend had more influence with him than me.

My dad stepped out of the way, which was our signal to take off and find her. We did not waste any time and went to the places I knew my mom was frequenting. I took him everywhere except to Big Daddy Wayne's house because I was scared. Unfortunately, when we didn't find her, I turned to Amir and confessed all.

Taking a deep breath I said, "She's probably where she was a few days ago."

He boldly said, "Okay, why didn't you tell me to go there first?"

I couldn't even face him. I could not even talk about what happened to me at that trashy place. I knew he must have thought very little of me, having to take me around to find my trashed and coked-out mother.

"You can talk to me," Amir said in a soothing voice.

I really didn't deserve this guy. His words and actions showed he wanted to fix my world. I was so happy I did not have to go through this alone. I did not want to do anything to push him away.

Turning toward the window, I said, "It's just so hard. I feel so embarrassed."

He took one hand off the steering wheel and put it on the back of my neck. I rolled my neck toward him and my face ended up cupped in his hand.

"Please tell me what happened, Hallie."

Wanting to connect, I said, "I'm not a drinker, but I went and found my mom and this guy ..."

I didn't want to finish, but Amir pulled the car into a parking lot and just had me talk to him. He was astounded when I told him my experience at the crack house. As soon as I finished telling him my story, he drove silently to Big Daddy Wayne's house. He was so disgusted. He told me to stay put.

I shouted, "I can't stay in the car."

Amir looked at me like I was nuts. "Absolutely not! What if that same guy sees you again? Men like you described take what they want. It won't be any good for you or your mom, and I'm certainly not gonna stand by and watch some guy try to rape you. It's just not going down like that. But if he pulls out a gun or a knife, or some of his boys jump me ... I mean, there's no good way that that could play out. I know what your mom looks like. Let me see if I can find her. Let me see if anyone knows if she's here. Lock the door. Keep your phone in your hand."

While Amir was gone, I could not relax. I wanted my mom to be there, but I knew if she was there she would degrade and debase herself to score some crack. I wondered why my father could not let her remain at our place, get some coffee in her system, sober her up, and talk to her like he used to do. I needed him to care. This was my mom, not just some trick trying to hustle us.

Amir came back and had his hands up. He didn't have to say a word. I knew she was not there. I felt the worry course through my veins, and it made me feel worse than my bout with alcohol from a few nights before.

"I'm sorry, she was not in there," he said. Amir shrugged.

"Yeah, I got that."

"Where else you wanna look?"

"I don't know anywhere else to look," I sighed.

I didn't want to go off on him, but I was frustrated. I was upset. I needed to calm down. I did not want to break.

"Why is this happening to me?" I screamed out. "Why do I feel so alone? My dad hates my mom, and my mom hates herself. We used to be a family. There ... there used to be love."

I was so into my own pain that I almost missed that Amir was teary-eyed himself. We ended up driving to a park. No one was there. I saw his eyes had care and concern in them. I knew deep down I wanted to feel real good. I put my hand on the back of his neck and pulled his face toward mine. I kissed him, and I was so into it. My tongue knew what to do. I started lifting my shirt. When it was off, his eyes twinkled. I kissed his neck. I was forgetting my pain, and I started unbuttoning his shirt.

Amir pulled back and said, "Wait, wait, wait. Hold up."

"What do you mean hold up? You said I'm not alone. Be with me."

"You're not alone. I'm right here."

I reached back over to him and said, "Then make me feel good, please."

"No, you're doing this for the wrong reasons. You want to dull the pain, but you have to understand that life is always going to throw curves. You can't turn to alcohol. You can't turn to sex. Those things are not going to make your life instantly better."

Trying to touch the muscles that were bulging from his chest to change his mind, I said,

"Come on. I want to feel better, but you know I care for you."

"Hallie, we haven't really talked about your drinking binge the other night. Hearing about all that you went through, I get it. That still wasn't a wise choice. I mean, guys at the party were looking like they wanted to tap you, and there are guys who won't take no for an answer."

I didn't care what he was saying. I wasn't listening. I straddled his lap and started kissing his ear. I took his hand and put it on my chest, but he did not caress me. I'm not saying I had watermelons, but I was nicely formed and burning for some skin-to-skin contact. I did not know what was wrong with the brother.

"You're not gay or anything?" I blurted.

Then he became angry. He made sure I was over on my side of his car. He huffed.

He sighed, "Hallie, you just don't get it."

"No, you just don't get it!" I yelled back at him. "All I wanted to do is have a little fun. Just take me home. I thought you could make me feel good. You're such a wimp. You won't even play football, jerk."

He didn't disrespect me, but he gave me a slight grunt, like he knew something that I did not know. At that point I did not care what it was. I could not stand him. I did not need him to do me any favors in terms of keeping my dignity. I needed him to honor my request and help me feel good. What use was he if he would not do that?

"You sure you don't mind taking extra time to teach me the routine again?" I said to Charli. I felt so guilty that she was spending so much free time with me. She had to go over everything with me multiple times. I was not the fastest learner. I tried getting the placement down, but I was bumping into everyone.

Charli said in a sweet voice, "When are you going to get that I love you, girl? Let's just break the routine up into thirds. We can go over the first half, really get that down, finish the middle, and then come back and do the end. Then later we can hook up with Brenton and Amir. Brenton says they're hanging out some now."

"What?" I exclaimed. "Why? Amir is a loner. He doesn't want friends. He makes it impossible to get to know him."

"From the stories he told Brenton, he's made a pretty good effort at trying to support you. I know firsthand that you can be high maintenance. So you might want to cut the brother some slack," Charli said, as she pushed play on the CD player.

Not only was Charli a dynamite dancer, she was also a really cool instructor. I didn't know if Cheertowne had dance, but she would be a great one to work with the little kids. She didn't treat me like I was different—you know, the one riding the special bus—but she accommodated my pace. Before I knew it, I had the first part down. Then she plopped down and put both of her hands on her head, as if she was exhausted.

I said, "Charli, I'm sorry. I know this has taken a lot out of you, having to do it over and over again. Though you like dancing, this might be excruciating to teach the same basic moves a million times over."

"Please, girl, it ain't even that at all. I'm captain, and I should work overtime with anyone on the squad who needs it. Can I ask you a question?" Charli inquired.

"Sure." I squinted and I wondered what was so heavy.

"Here's the thing, how do you always stay so fired up, so excited? I mean, yeah, lately you've been going through about this thing with your mom, but your mom has been tripping for years, and you've always seemed to hold it in. My dad has only been out of our house for a few weeks. I can't even sleep at night. Can you please tell me how you do it?"

I plopped down beside her. "I don't know if I *am* doing it. I've been feeling like my life has been unraveling lately, and I'm not able to keep it together. I guess I just pretended to hold it in. I never really felt good enough, you know? Would a mother abandon a perfect child? Well, my mom abandoned me, and I haven't felt good about myself since. That's no way to be. No way to feel. That's no way to think. Being down on yourself only makes you unattractive because the insecurities come out in many ways. Your grades suffer. You don't care how you dress. You get self-conscious about how you dance. Charli Black, you can't force your parents to work out their problems."

"Tell me about it," she agreed.

"But you can be there for them. Just keep telling yourself it has nothing to do with you.

Hold your head up high, keep your confidence, and you'll learn to adapt. I've got a feeling in your case it's gonna work itself out. Keep moving and don't focus on the drama," I said. We hugged. And I realized that maybe I should follow my own advice.

Later that day I was practicing with my stunting group. Eva, Ella, Randal, and I were having trouble keeping our stunt up. As we got ready for our first competition and we kept practicing, our pyramid was the one that kept falling. So we got together outside of practice to work on it. Randal's tiny self was on top. Eva and Ella were the bases, and I was the back spot. Randal was really having a time with the switch up where you start from the ground and switch legs before stopping the stunt. Two people were to hold one foot, and then they had to let go and grab the opposite foot. If the person up top did not stay tight, they'd fall.

When Ella and Eva dropped Randal for the third time, Randal sat down in the middle of the mat and said, "I don't wanna do it anymore. I don't care about doing it. You will have to find someone else to put up. Try Hallie."

Eva was about to go off, and Ella was about to tell her not to worry about it and that she'd get it. Randal needed more than someone being over-the-top mean, but she didn't need someone telling her what she wanted to hear because that wouldn't make it happen either. I told them both to take a break.

I sat down beside Randal and said, "Girl, you can do this."

"I just like tumbling across the front, but since I can't do fulls and layouts, Charli is chosen to flip across the front. Now I have to go up in the air. I wish I was more like you."

I started coughing at that moment. What in the world could Randal be talking about ... she admired me? Uh-uh! I was so taken aback.

"You got this desire," she said. She could tell that I thought she was mistaken and possibly a little crazy.

"What do you mean by desire?" I asked dubiously.

"I mean, you want to be a cheerleader. You want to master every part of it. You're fearless."

Disagreeing, I said, "No, I have a mental block."

"Yeah, but that's only in tumbling. You wanna get it. I don't want to do some of this stuff. I just wish I cared as much as you did. You're like the poster child for cheerleading, for goodness' sake. Where does that drive come from? To keep going and working and trying and pushing. Everybody's been giving you a hard time on the squad for not holding up your end, but truth be told, there's so many of us who don't have things right. Some folks don't have tight arms. Some girls' jumps are a little off. It's just obvious because you can't tumble, but we all need to be on point if we wanna win, and I just wanna know how you don't ever let any of that get to you."

"Cheering is a dream come true. When it comes to this mental block thing, I'm trying to push past it. I'm going to be honest with you, I'm not all the way there. But I got to deal with myself about that and face my fears head on. The sky is the limit for me, and the sky is the limit for you too. I'm not only going to cheer for myself, but I wanna do my part for the team. You must ask yourself, how badly do you want this, and who are you really doing it for? And if you got a firm grasp on why this is important to you, you'll figure out how to master it. I've been going to this gym, and I didn't wanna tell anybody, so please don't share it yet. They can help you get better at this stuff."

"So do have your tumbling?" Randal asked the magic question.

"Just pray for me," I responded and she nodded.

I went out to get a sip of water. The twins met me and just kept staring at me. I stared back but could not understand.

"What? Do I have something on my face?" I asked.

Eva said, "Nah, we just saw you over there talking to Randal. You got a gift, girl."

"You really do," Ella replied.

"I'm confused. I know I got a mouth on me," I said, knowing they always called me the big-mouthed one.

"Yeah, lately you've been really tamed," Ella said. "But you are never mean with what you say to people. I like that you have purpose, but you aren't blunt."

Eva said, "And I know I need to learn how to be more diplomatic. I'm just not trying to be so political like my sister, sugarcoating everything."

"Ha-ha-ha," Ella said. "Though she's right, Hallie. I hate that I'm so nice. People think I'm a push-over." She looked at Eva and rolled her eyes. "But I never want to be so mean to people. I like a good balance between the two of us. You are that balance. Actually, you are the balance between all five of us. I mean, Randal barely says anything, so the best time to hang out with her is when you don't want to be bothered, and Charli—"

Like a twin finishes the other's thoughts, Eva cut in and said, "And Charli's so high society. Sometimes I wonder if she can relate to people who aren't perfect. She would just bounce. We love you, girl. That's all. So come on, let's get back out there."

We all walked back to the mats. I realized that I was so hard on myself because I felt inferior to my friends. After spending time with all four of them, I realized they admired something about me too. Knowing they saw something great in me kept me motivated to keep doing what I was doing, stay in my lane, and be proud of Hallie Ray. I had it going on too. How cool.

It was the second game of the season, and we were 1–0 and so were our rivals, the MLK Tigers. The place was jumping. Before kickoff there was so much hype. The bands were battling. The dancers were trying to outdo each other, and the crowds were yelling back and forth to see who made the most noise. There was absolutely no place in the world I wanted to be more than in front of our home crowd doing my thang.

Right before kickoff Coach Woods came up to me and killed my joyous mood by saying, "So it's been a couple of weeks. Where are you with the required skills?"

"I've got it," I said to her, knowing that I did know how to tumble, but I had only been working with my girls on our routine and stunting.

"You've got it?" she said, wanting reassurance. "Wow, okay. I'm proud of you, Hallie. I knew you could do it."

"Thanks, Coach, I won't let you down." I nervously walked back into position.

I didn't know if Coach believed me or had to test me, but she said, "Girls, I'm going to play our competition music. Mark the stunts, but I want to make sure you guys have the moves."

I knew everyone had the moves but me. Charli worked with me, and now I needed to show her I could do it. When the music played, I did my thing as if we were in front of judges getting scored. As soon as we were done, she gave me a thumbs-up. Thankfully, I passed the coach's test—the first one anyway.

We got crushed in the first quarter. There were two quick, long passes, a weak left side, and just like that we were behind. Wax had the potential of being a D1 running back, but even he was getting stuffed. When defense was called to get back out on the field, they let a TD get scored off another long bomb.

Lions' fans held their breaths in the second quarter. We did nothing with our offensive possession, but when defense got out on the field, there was an interception. Our stand went nuts. Not only did the boy catch the ball, but he was ditching and dodging the opposing players. He took the ball in for a score. Our sidelines burst with excitement.

"Amir Knight with the interception and touchdown. Go Lions! Amir, where have you been all our lives?" the announcer joked.

Hearing the loudspeaker, I froze. I knew I heard the name right, but that couldn't be! Was Amir now playing football? Ever since I'd passionately attacked him, we had not spoken. He didn't call me, and I wasn't picking up the phone to call him. Thinking on it, I realized that he had not been at Cheertowne. Was it because he was on the football team? Now everything was making sense.

We made the extra point, and after the kickoff we were back on defense. I wanted to cheer. I wanted to yell. I wanted to shake my tushie. However, there was something in me that ignored the crowd. I turned and looked at the field. On the first play of that series, there was another long throw and it was intercepted again, but not because the quarterback didn't throw it to his man. Amir came clear across field and took it. Though he didn't take it in that time for a touchdown, he was still amazing.

The announcer screamed, "Amir Knight with another interception."

Our quarterback, Blake Strong, came in and threw a touchdown pass to Landon King. Just like that we were back in the game, tied with the Tigers 14–14. I was still tripping Amir was ballin'.

Charli came over to me and started jumping up and down, "Did you see that? Do you know who that was? Two interceptions! The boy is bad. Oh my gosh!"

Eva came rushing over to me. "Why didn't you tell us your boy could play?"

"Right," Ella said. "He's got swag, girl."

Randal chimed in. "You told us he wasn't in any activities. Your Amir went from bench-warmer to stud."

Throwing up my pom-poms I said, "No, honestly y'all, I didn't know he was playing football."

I looked over at Charli who had a very bold grin. She knew something. I should have known when she said Brenton was hanging with Amir that there was more to it.

"What?" she giggled.

"Did you know? You said he was hanging out with Brenton. Is this why? Are they teammates now?" I asked Charli.

"Yes."

"Uh, why didn't you tell me?" I wondered.

Charli blurted out, "He didn't want you to know."

"Huh?" Eva said, "That's crazy, why not? She loves football. Maybe he thought he wouldn't be any good."

I chimed in, "No, that's not what it is. He hates me. We're not talking anymore. We had a big blowup. I guess he felt that it was none of my business. I'm happy for him though. He is really good. He should be out there, and that's where we needed him. So we've got a secondary."

"Look at you, acting like you don't care," Charli said. She gave me a little shove. "He likes you, girl, I know he does. Brenton says he talks about you all the time."

"Ladies, quit yapping your mouths and get out there on the field," Coach Woods shouted. "It's halftime. You need to be able to walk straight on when the players go off so you don't waste time on the clock. The band has to play after you are introduced!"

The team was running past us, and out of all the ninety-something players, I immediately spotted Amir. I did not know if he wanted me to find him or what because his helmet was still on. It was like we had magnetic chemistry. We were just drawn together. Amir must have wanted to see me because he stopped running and took off his helmet.

I asked, "You're playing ball now?"

He turned the tables on me. "So you're flipping now?"

"Amir, get on to that locker room. There's no time for socializing," Coach Strong called out.

The cheerleaders lined up in alphabetical order for the introductions. With the last name Ray, I was at the end. When it came time for us to tumble, I just knew I could do it. I had been practicing at the gym. Mentally I was ready. My girls believed in me, and I believed in myself. Even Amir cared enough to give me a psychological boost. I knew he meant it if he was out there doing what I thought he could do. Now I needed to get out there and do what he knew I could. When my name was called, I just stood there. Nobody had me tied up. Nobody was laughing. Yeah, it seemed as if everything was going in slow motion.

I heard Charli call out, "You got this, Hallie, flip."

Ella said, "Come on, Hallie, just tumble. You can do it, sweetie."

Salty Eva mouthed, "If you don't tumble ..."

Randal smiled and crossed her fingers. Running was not an option. Sink or swim, I had to stand there. All the hard work did not matter. All the positive words meant nothing. All the trying was pointless because when it came time to show up, I shut down and could not do it.

CHAPTER 7

Dreams Realized

When we came off the field, Coach Woods walked right over to me, and I felt my dream of being a varsity cheerleader slipping from my grasp. She had given me leeway. She had put me on her team though I did not have all the skills. She has taken a chance on me. She had pumped me up. She told me I could do it, but when it came time to show her that I could, I failed.

Before she said anything, I exclaimed, "So do I need to turn in my pom-poms right now and bring my uniform next week after I wash it or what?"

Coach Woods smirked, "Oh, I'm not going to let you off that easily. You told me you could do it. You might need a little more time, but I'm holding you to it. We're counting on you, Hallie." She lifted my chin. "I believe in you."

I could have hugged her at that moment. The rest of the cheerleaders came up to me and encouraged me as well. It was like someone told them that negative reinforcement was not the way to get me to comply with what they needed. As a person who needed words of affirmation, they were going all out with kind phrases. Emotion was taking me over.

I had done many flips in the gym, so I knew I could do it. Since the team did not give up on me, I was going to overcome my fear and perform. I had to be successful. I had to conquer what was in my way. I had to move what was blocking me.

"Go get yourself something to drink, get ready for second half, come back out, and be the best cheerleader I have," Coach Woods said. "What you do is contagious because you are so enthusiastic. Trust what is in your heart and relax. We'll worry about all the rest of this stuff next week." She gave me a quick hug and walked away to handle some other small drama.

After every home game, some sport or club hosted a dance. Our principal, Dr. Sapp, said as long as we did not lose our minds and acted like we had some common sense, we could keep having parties. There was something different about this particular party. I walked in with my girls. All heads turned to look at us, but this time I did not feel like I didn't belong. I was not envious or jealous anymore of the attention my girls were getting. Since my head was held high, I got some whistles my way. I was the last girl standing alone two weeks ago when all my friends were asked to dance. However, before we even got situated, Amir came out of nowhere.

The fine dude said, "Excuse me, ladies, you mind if I take your girl away for a second?"

Eva pushed me into him. "No, big baller, dance with her."

"Eva!" I blushed.

"If that's okay with you, of course," he asked me.

Quickly I clarified, "Yes, that's great."

My girls oohed and aahed as I walked arm and arm with Amir to the dance floor. It was a slow song. I had to admit, my heart started racing as he put his arms around my waist. It took our bodies no time to get in sync with the music and with each other. He pulled back just a little so that our eyes would meet.

"I don't want to play any games with you," Amir admitted to me. "It's been killing me not to talk to you and tell you all that I've been going through."

Not getting the magnitude of what he wanted to say, I said, "Yeah, I am surprised you were out on the football field. Please tell me you didn't think you needed to play football for me. You had my heart anyway."

It was important to me that Amir knew I wasn't shallow. Even though we hadn't been talking, I had still thought of him. He did not need to be a baller on the field to be the baller of my heart.

Seeing him smile, he said, "I know. Turns out you were right. Football is in my blood, and I needed to try playing."

"I'm sure your dad must have been really proud," I said, knowing they were disconnected. "Was he here tonight?"

Amir looked away. Something was not right. It seemed I'd upset him.

"What's wrong? Did I say something?" I asked with concern.

"That's been a part of my drama. I wanted to reach out to you because I thought that you would understand."

"Why, because my life is so screwed because of my mom?" I uttered.

"Yeah, did you find her? Have y'all talked to her?"

I shook my head and looked away. Then I realized what he wanted to talk to me about did not involve my drama. The fact that he wanted to open up to me meant a lot.

"Do you want to go somewhere and talk?" I said when the song ended.

He shook his head and took my hand. We went over to a corner. He leaned in real close and whispered in my ear.

"I told you a long time ago that I felt like an outsider in my own home. Do you remember that?" he asked. "When you talked to me about playing football, I gave you a hard time about it because my dad had instilled in me that football was for chumps. But I didn't really think that. I thought some guys on this team didn't have any work ethic. I did realize that I have skills at the safety position, and I wanted to try them out. My dad wasn't for that. There was a lot of drama in my house. All that to say, it came out that … he's not even my biological dad."

I was so shocked and hurt for Amir. He was so close to me that our lips touched. He backed away for a second.

Breathing heavily he said, "I don't even want to bother you with this."

"No, no," I said, as I pulled him closer to me. "Talk to me. It's no bother."

"Are you sure?"

"I mean, you don't have to tell me what you don't want to."

"Thanks," Amir said. He touched my cheek and continued with his story. "My mom tipped out on my dad when they were having problems and here I am. I guess he has some fault in this because he cheated first. She was just getting back at him. My dad has known my entire life. She was never trying to cover it up to him, and they agreed he would raise me as his own.

Problem was he never dealt with his anger and has made me feel like an outcast all my life. So when I found out I wasn't his, I felt like I didn't have to live up to his expectations anymore. My mom signed the necessary forms, and I came on out for Coach Strong's team. I have been on the team for a week."

"Are you okay?" I said, never wanting anything heavy to be in Amir's heart.

I knew what it was like to have parent drama, but I could not imagine it being sprung on you after sixteen years of thinking one person was your parent and learning they had no blood connection to you at all. This was too much.

"I'm dealing with it, but I guess it made me realize things that were important in my life, and I want one of those things to be you. I've been with girls for the wrong reason, and I just respect you more than that."

"What are you saying, Amir?" I asked, truly wanting to know and not assume anything.

"I want you to be my girl."

At that moment I couldn't hear any more music. The spotlight was on us. I had always wanted a guy who cared about me. I wanted him to be cute. I wanted him to have swagger. I wanted it to be real. Feeling Amir's lips against mine, he could tell that my answer to his question was yes.

When I got home later that evening, I was hesitant to walk into my house. Greta's car was in the driveway. Instead of just using my key, I was more comfortable ringing the bell. No need for a repeat.

"Hey, baby girl," my dad said, as he gave me a kiss on the cheek and did not even question my method of entering the house. "You have fun tonight?"

"Yes, sir," I said, peeping into the house before I stepped inside.

"Don't trip. Come on in. Hopefully, you're not tired. Greta and I wanted to talk to you. She made some hot chocolate. Maybe we can all sit around and gab."

I thought to myself, "All sit around and gab? Okay, Dad, what is going on with you?" Though I had come to the realization that his girlfriend meant something to him and was not going anywhere, I did not want to cosign on the whole brand new family idea. I only had less than two years to be in this house. If he and Greta could just hold out until then, whatever they wanted to do I would be fine with, but I did not want him moving her in before then. If us sitting around and having a conversation was going to mean that I had to act like I was okay with it all, he could count me out.

I threw my hands up and sharply said, "Dad, just talk to your girl. You guys enjoy the cocoa. I can get my stuff and spend the night with Charli or something. Just give me a second and I'll be out. I don't want to get in y'all's way."

I was not trying to be a brat, really. Greta headed me off and handed me a cup of cocoa as she exited the kitchen. It had whipped cream on it. It was steaming and looked delicious.

"This is for you," she smiled.

I just looked at the cup. Though I wanted it badly, I could not take her little bribe. We were not friends, and I was not going to be tricked.

Greta tried handing me the enticing drink and said, "Please, Hallie. I really care about your father, and he cares about you. I just wanted to apologize for us getting off to such a rough start. I want to tell you I am not trying to take your mom's place. I know I can never do that. Meeting you, I understand why you're your father's pride and joy. You're beautiful. You got savvy."

When she used a word that was current and something I use with my friends, I was taken aback. I was surprised in a good way. Maybe Greta was hipper than I thought, but I still didn't *want* to like her. As I saw the whipped cream melting before my eyes, I just took it. No need to be rude, so I went and sat down on the couch and started sipping. The mixture of vanilla, marshmallows, and whipped cream in the chocolatey hot milk was so soothing. It was the perfect drink to have when coming in from the chilly fall night.

"Sweetheart," my dad said to me, as he took my free hand, "I love you. Whatever is important to you is important to me. I know you are worried about your mom. So tomorrow I would like for us to go and try to find her. See if we can put her in rehab."

"Oh my gosh, Dad! You would do that?" I cried.

"I would because I love you that much. I need you to have peace of mind and be happy with your life."

"I know you don't want me to come," Greta said with teary eyes. "But I am truly concerned about your mom, and I want her to get the help that she needs. Please know I'm not trying to stand in the way of that. I'm here, however, and I can assist."

I could not hold back my emotions. I knew Greta had to have talked to my dad about helping me find my mom. My dad did a complete turnaround, which almost never happens. That only had to be because of her influence, and if she could help him see that my mom needed us, then maybe I needed to open up my eyes and see that my dad needed Greta.

"I'm going to go to bed now so we can get up in the morning and find Mom," I said.

I turned back around and took my dad's hand. He smiled. I embraced Greta. He smiled wider.

"You two enjoy each other. Thanks," I said. And I meant it.

I looked back and saw Greta crying silently. Seeing her emotion was really sweet. I moved her by my simple actions and words. Because I was not bitter, I felt like a burden I did not even know was on me was lifted too. It was weird and certainly unexplainable, but it was real. By not being so hard-hearted, I could feel.

It took my dad and I all of an hour to find my mom. I took him straight to the last place I knew her to be. This time she was there. She was shriveled up in a ball, holding her legs, and rocking back and forth. She had on Daisy Dukes and a bra. It was sixty degrees. Immediately my dad took off his light jacket. She seemed in such a trance that I did not know if she could understand what I was saying or not.

"Ugh, I don't know where you trying to go with her, but you ain't taking her nowhere. She owe me some moola, money, dough. Wassup?" the same joker who tried to assault me said to my father.

I certainly did not want to tell my dad what that dude had done to me. He would have killed him. I didn't want my dad in trouble over a low-life like that. He gave the thug some money, and we got my mom in the car.

Greta had called a drug rehabilitation center that had an available bed. My dad shelled out dough again to pay for Mom's slot. My mom was shivering from the cold, and it tore me up to see her so shaken and frail. My dad said she was having withdrawals from not having drugs in her system. Probably her pusher would not give her any because she owed him, I guess. She was pretty close to stroking out.

Seeing her so weak as my father checked her in, I realized I was growing up. I could not keep thinking that the world had done me wrong because my mom chose to love drugs more than she loved me. My dad and I were getting her help. Now she was going to have to make the choice to take it.

In a loving manner I boldly said, "Mom, I know this is going to be hard. This is like the third time you've been to a place like this. But this is the first time I've been allowed to come along. I need you to do this for me. I need you to care enough about *you* so you can get well for *you* because *I* am going to be okay."

"I ... I ... I love you, Hal. I love you, baby. I'm going to make it this time. I'm going to make it this time," she mumbled.

I nodded, letting her know I was counting on her to keep her word. Then she collapsed in the nurse's arms. My dad did not want to leave, but I tugged on his arm.

I said, "It's okay, Dad. You've done more than your share to help her. All I could ever ask of you is for you to help her this last time. For you to do that means everything. They said we can come and visit her in a week."

"I'm proud of you, Hallie," my dad said.

"Why?"

"Because you told your mom the truth even though it was tough. Though you can never turn your back on people you love, sometimes you need to cut them loose. We can't just give her a fish. We have to teach her how to fish."

"I don't understand," I said.

Walking to the front door, he explained, "Just an old proverb that says, 'If you give a man a fish, he will eat for a day.' You know that fish you gave him? He's going to put it over the fire. Maybe put a little salt and pepper on it and grub."

I laughed.

" 'But if you teach a man *how* to fish, he will eat for a lifetime.' He can come to the water. Clear his mind. Cast his net. Feed his family. Have self pride. Realize his own dreams and goals. Bringing your mom here can teach her how to fish, but she's got to want to learn."

I nodded. I hoped she would learn. We walked out of the rehab center, giving her a chance to do just that. I felt good that our job was done.

"Why didn't you just flip the other night?" Lexus asked. It was Sunday, and I was warming up for tumbling at Cheertowne. "I've seen you in here doing it a million times. You get under the lights and freeze up. Why? You got the skills, and your calves can hold you up."

In my mind I started to ask her, "Why in the world do you care? I know you want Amir, but I don't want you to bug me. I'm not trying to rub our relationship in your face. So just go. Ugh."

But I stood there, counted to three, and was real calm, hoping that the other trainer would come out so I could practice.

"I don't know why you're looking around. I'm the one who's going to work with you today," Lexus barked.

"No, I'm going to work with her," Amir shocked us both and said.

Lexus vented, "You don't even work here anymore."

"Oh, but I prefer to work with him, and my money gets a say," I said in an excited tone. Seeing my boyfriend for the first time since we made a commitment to date each other made me blush from head to toe.

"It's a liability issue. He doesn't work here," the bossy girl said. She would not let up.

"Lexus, come here for a second," the owner of the gym called out from his office.

If looks could kill, Amir and I would both be dead. When she did not walk off, he grabbed my hand, and we went to another part of the gym. I looked back, and Lexus was still staring.

"She is unstable," I said to him. I was dying to kiss him but there were lots of little girls swarming around us. I had savvy and was not going to be inappropriate.

"She's got some issues, but just ignore her," he said as we faced one another. "I was hoping you would be here."

"I've got to tumble, Amir. The craziest thing is all the pressure I felt on me not being able to tumble … Well, I don't feel it anymore, but more than ever before I've got to tumble."

"And I think that's the first step to getting you there. You've got to want to. So let's go."

Amir held out his arm. When he counted to three I felt comfortable and was flipping. It just became routine. His arm was there and I was flipping. I did not feel his arm on my back after eight flips, but he assured me it was there. After the fifteenth time when I looked up he was five steps back, and though they were not big steps, he was not helping me. I was doing it on my own.

"So all I'm saying is we have an away game Friday, and when they introduce the cheerleaders, every single one of them is going to show out," Amir said confidently.

I rolled my neck and hips. "And how about the football team … are we going to win?" I asked.

"Like you even got to ask," he said.

After we wrestled for a few seconds, I stood and said, "Hey, are you okay? You know, all the stuff with your dad?"

"Can't worry about what you can't control in this life, Hallie. You've got to focus on the positive stuff you got going on so you can go somewhere in life. You can't be bogged down with stress and worry. Worrying about the negative things holds you back. You can't live. You can't keep going. You know that all you need is to just keep jumping."

"You're amazing," I said to him.

"Don't give me too much credit."

"No, I'm serious. You don't just look at life from your point of view. The reason why you're able to keep jumping is because you're able to understand how the other person feels. You have empathy. Not many of us put ourselves in the other person's shoes. Yeah, we want to walk in their shoes when we think they have it going on, but we don't want to walk in the mud they have to go through to get on top."

The week flew by. Amir and I could not hang out because I had cheerleading practice and tumbling practice after that. And there was still homework to be done. He had football practice and meetings with the coaches after school so he could learn the plays he was behind on.

On game night we rode the bus with the defense and when I passed by Amir, he touched my arm and smiled.

"Have a good game tonight," I said to him before Coach Woods told us to keep it moving.

"Did you hear him?" Charli said.

"No."

"He said he has a feeling y'all both will have a good night. What does he mean by that? You getting lucky, girl?" she said to me.

I just laughed. When we were sitting in the back, I asked Charli how things were going with her parents.

She hugged me and said, "Thanks for asking. I appreciate that you care. My parents are dating other people. That's all I can say, but I haven't fallen apart. I am taking your advice on not letting it affect me. Whatever they do, I know they still love me."

"That's what I'm talking about," I said.

Ella and Eva were the cutest twins. I did not know that many twins, but they had to be the best ones in the world. I gave them both kisses.

Eva said, "Ew!"

And Ella said, "Thank you!"

They were so predictable. Their dad had a whole new family and was about to get married, and I knew it was eating the two of them up. But the sugar and spice combo would get them through it, and I was happy to be there for both of them. Randal came on the bus late. There were no more seats.

I got up and said, "Here, you sit here."

"I don't want to take your seat," Randal said shyly.

I said, "You're not. You sit in the middle, and I'll just be on the end."

"Thank you for caring. I would have had a panic attack if I had to ask anybody to slide in so tight," Randal said.

I loved those four girls so much. To be uncomfortable on a bus ride was nothing. We were supposed to blow out the team we were playing. But in the first half we were down 14–7.

Amir and I passed each other when he was jogging to the locker room. The cheerleaders were going to be introduced in the center of the field. I winked at him. When the announcer called my name, not only did I do two back handsprings, I also did a full.

My team went wild. They all came running to me and lifted me up like I had scored the winning touchdown. It felt amazing leaving all my fears behind. It felt wonderful going for the gusto. It was marvelous knowing that I was not going to have to turn in my pom-poms.

When the cheerleaders ran off, I saw Amir and jogged over to him. I had been on a crazy rollercoaster the last few weeks, and I am actually somebody who is terrified of rollercoasters. It was like somebody had pushed me on and said just enjoy it. But I could not loosen up. I could not let go. I could not change the twists and turns, so I screamed and fought it. It was no fun until I relaxed. It was not until I took my hands off the bars, raised them in the air, and just went with the flow that I could conquer my fear. I knew that if I just kept riding, kept living, kept trying, and kept jumping I could do anything.

Amir tried to act like it was no big deal and said, "I'm glad you saw me because if Coach knows I'm not in that locker room …"

I put my hand over his lips and kissed his cheek. "Thank you for helping me. From the very beginning you told me I could do it."

"My savvy, sweet Hallie Ray, no need to thank me. You had it in you all the time. Be proud of yourself now that you've got your dreams realized."